FIGMENT, YOUR DOG, SPEAKING

LAURA HAWKINS

Houghton Mifflin Company

Boston 1991

J

Library of Congress Cataloging-in-Publication Data

Hawkins, Laura.
  Figment, your dog, speaking / Laura Hawkins.
    p. cm.
  Summary: A talking dog with a knack for changing people's lives
helps fourth grader Marcella deal with her tendency to tell wild
stories to get attention.
  ISBN 0-395-57032-8
  [1. Dogs—Fiction. 2. Honesty—Fiction.] I. Title.
PZ7.H313517Fi 1991   91-10880
[Fic]—dc20   CIP
                              AC

Copyright © 1991 by Laura Hawkins

Printed in the United States of America

AGM 10 9 8 7 6 5 4 3 2 1

With love to my Terrific Three—
Mother, Jennifer and Erin

1

When Mrs. Crandall asked Marcella Starbuckle to stay after school, Marcella answered loud enough for the whole fourth-grade class to hear:

"As long as I'm home by four o'clock. That's when the President is going to call me."

Everyone in the room groaned, including Mrs. Crandall.

"If you don't believe me," Marcella said, "come to my house at four o'clock."

"So you can tell another lie?" Tammy Collins asked, smirking.

"We're too busy anyway," Ryan Soetart said. "Everybody but you's been invited to the White House at four o'clock. That's what the President's going to call you about."

The classroom thundered with laughter. Then the last bell pierced the din and a stream of buzzing boys and girls flowed out of the room, some chanting, "Liar, liar, pants on fire!"

When the room was empty, Mrs. Crandall's green eyes rolled up and rested on Marcella. She jerked a little breath and then, as if she had changed her mind about speaking, she sat silent a moment. Finally, she stood up.

"Marcella, I have another note for you to give to your parents." She plucked the folded piece of paper from the corner of her desk and extended it to Marcella. "It's about the excuses you keep giving me for not having your homework."

Marcella knew "excuses" was another word for lies, but she didn't mind. She liked Mrs. Crandall. She liked to guess which of Mrs. Crandall's five different matching earrings-and-necklace sets her teacher would wear on any given day. White, clear glass, red, blue, or green?

Marcella played a game with herself each morning while she walked alone to school. If she guessed Mrs. Crandall's jewelry for the day, she rewarded herself after school with an extra cookie. She especially liked it, too, when Mrs. Crandall asked her to stay after school and talk. She always took an extra cookie for that, too.

Today she would get two extra cookies, one for staying after school and one for guessing Mrs. Crandall's green jewelry, although it was cheating a little, since it was Saint Patrick's Day and everyone wore green on Saint Patrick's Day. All except Marcella. She purposefully wore blue so she would get pinched. Only nobody would pinch her!

"I'm not wearing green today, Mrs. Crandall," Marcella blurted out.

"No, you're not. But I'm afraid to ask why not."

Marcella smiled. It was fun thinking of something to say that would make Mrs. Crandall afraid.

"Because my dog ate my green skirt. He ate the matching green belt that goes with it."

Marcella said that because she thought Mrs. Crandall, being a jewelry person, would be interested in accessories such as belts.

"My dog looks a lot like that dog's picture in the newspaper you read during current events."

During current-events time, Mrs. Crandall had read an ad from the *Riverview Chronicle* about someone's lost dog. When she thought about it, Marcella decided the missing black and white shepherd-spaniel would be the kind of dog she

3

would own and the kind that would eat a green skirt.

She supposed, after going days without food, the dog might be hungry enough to eat a blue dress, too. Specifically, the blue dress her mother had brought back to Marcella from a business trip to California.

Marcella didn't like that blue dress. She didn't like California because her mother was always going there on business trips. Marcella hated business even worse than California. It was always taking her parents away to places sometimes farther than dumb old California!

"And I suppose, Marcella," Mrs. Crandall said, her face tightening, "that your dog ate your current event. That's why you didn't have one today?"

Mrs. Crandall was losing her patience. Pretty soon she would stop talking. Marcella didn't want that to happen, so this time she told the truth.

"No, Mrs. Crandall. My father took the newspaper with him on his business trip to Chicago." That was the real reason she didn't have a chance to get a current event from the newspaper. Marcella was hating Chicago even worse than California.

Mrs. Crandall seemed to like the newspaper-that-got-away story just fine. The lines around her mouth disappeared. She seemed relieved to hear about the forgotten current event. In fact, Marcella thought she saw Mrs. Crandall smile.

"Well, Mrs. Crandall, it's almost four o'clock," Marcella said, glancing at the big clock above the blackboard. "I'd better get home before my dog eats the telephone."

2

When Marcella stepped outside the Riverview Elementary School, the Fantastic Four were huddled together, whispering. The Fantastic Four were four girls in Marcella's class who did everything together. They walked, talked, and even went to the bathroom together. Marcella thought it was a little ridiculous to have to have somebody to go to the bathroom with, but she thought it might be kind of nice to always have somebody to talk to.

"Hey, Marcella," Tammy Collins, the leader, called to her. "Want to join our search party?"

Marcella shook her head. She knew from past experience that when the Fantastic Four asked her to join them they were only doing it to make fun of her and then run away.

"I have to get home," Marcella said, and shuffled past them.

Before she knew it, the Fantastic Four were

walking one on each side of her and two at her back. Marcella walked faster.

"Don't you want two hundred dollars?" Libby Grimes asked.

"You have two hundred dollars?" Marcella slowed down a bit.

"No," Tammy Collins answered, "but if we find that missing dog, we each get that much. There's a thousand-dollar reward!"

"Weren't you listening during current events?" Linda Cappanelli asked.

"Marcella never listens," Jill Kramer shouted in Marcella's ear, as if she were deaf.

"Ow! Stop yelling in my ear." Marcella clamped a hand to the side of her head.

Tammy Collins marched away from the group. "Come on, you guys. Marcella wouldn't know where to find that dog. We're wasting our time."

When the others followed Tammy, Marcella called to them, "I know where he is all right. But I'm not going to tell."

The Fantastic Four stopped in their tracks and turned around to face Marcella. "She's lying," Tammy Collins said.

"Yeah, we can't trust her," Linda said.

"Wait a minute, you guys," Libby Grimes called.

"We're supposed to follow every lead, remember?"

"Marcella's not a lead," Tammy said, smirking. "She's a red herring."

"What's a red herring?" Libby wanted to know.

"And you call yourself a detective?" Tammy chastised Libby. "A red herring is somebody in a mystery who leads you on a wild-goose chase."

"Wrong," Marcella called. "I'm a blue herring." Couldn't Tammy Collins see she was wearing a blue dress? She must be blind!

"Well, I think she might be able to help us," Libby said.

Marcella always had liked Libby Grimes better than the other three Fantastic Fours. Libby never called Marcella names or made faces at her. She knew how to get her way without being mean like Tammy.

"Tell us where we can find the dog, and I'll invite you to my birthday party in two weeks," Libby said to Marcella, the other three girls standing in back of her.

"No you won't," Marcella challenged her. "You'll never send an invitation. You'll say you forgot."

"I'll bring you an invitation tomorrow," Libby Grimes promised.

"Then I'll tell you where the missing dog is tomorrow."

"You'll tell us today," Tammy Collins said, her face scrunching up. "Or we'll follow you everywhere."

"Good. I'm going home." Marcella started walking. She glanced back over her shoulder to see if the Fantastic Four were following her. They weren't. So she turned and called back to them. "I'm not going home. I'm going right to where the dog is."

That made the Fantastic Four chase after her. Marcella loved it. The Fantastic Four were good at walking and talking and going to the bathroom together, but they weren't as good as she was at running. She was the winged messenger Mercury!

Marcella ran fast and hard. Instead of her pants being on fire, it felt as if her lungs were on fire.

She cut through alleys and zigzagged in and out of yards until she was certain she'd lost the Fantastic Four. Some Fantastic Four they were!

Gasping for breath, Marcella flung herself against the workshop-garage door of Benny Slocum. Benny was a bear of a man with a hooded forehead that shaded blinking, pale blue eyes. He walked slowly and talked slowly. Everyone in Riverview called him "The Retard." All except for Marcella. Marcella called him Benny Boo, though never to his face, because Benny was so easily scared by things he didn't understand.

The thing that had scared Benny the most was when his father died a month ago. After that happened, Benny was more scared of more things than ever before. Benny was especially scared of going to live with his older brother. Benny said it was because his brother might die someday, too!

Marcella had met Benny Boo one day after school when she had nothing better to do than take a long, scenic walk home. She had found him fishing aluminum cans out of alley trash bins. "You won't tell on me, will you?" Benny Boo had asked Marcella. "Some people get mad. Me taking their cans. They call the police!"

Marcella thought about it a minute. "I won't tell," she'd said. "As long as you tell me what you do with them." Marcella was thinking she might want to collect cans herself. It might be something to fill her time since her parents were never home till late.

Benny Boo told her how he sold the cans to a man who paid money for them. "He melts them down. Makes new cans. They get used all over again. Come on. I'll show you."

That's when Benny Boo had led her to the garage in back of his tiny house. A mountain of cans was piled inside that garage. But Benny Boo didn't even point them out to her. He waddled over to an old refrigerator at the back. He opened it up and took out a can of soda pop. "Here. You see? This one's a new one. Made out of a bunch of cans I collected months ago." Benny Boo smiled. He seemed awfully proud of that brand-new soda-pop can, as if he'd made it himself or something. "Go ahead. Take it. Long as you give me back the can when you're done."

Marcella took the grape soda and pushed back the pop top. She swallowed a long drink and smiled at Benny Boo. That's when Benny Boo's eyes started blinking again, and he asked her, "You won't call the police, will you?"

"Call the police? Why would I call the police?"

"Some kids say they'll call the police."

"When you give them a free soda?" Marcella asked, puzzled.

"Yeah." Benny Boo nodded, his eyes bigger. "They say I give them poison."

Marcella looked down suspiciously at the can she'd been drinking from. "Why do they say that?"

Benny Boo rubbed the back of his big head with his mammoth hand. His face clouded. "Because . . . because . . ." His whole body tensed in search of the answer to Marcella's question. "I don't know," he finally said. "I don't know!"

Marcella knew. She knew how much fun lying could be sometimes, especially when someone believes everything you say.

"Uh-oh," Benny Boo said, glancing down at his watch. "It's time for 'Mr. Ed.' "

Then he had left Marcella standing there, pop can in her hand, and shuffled out of the garage, disappearing inside his house to watch his favorite TV show.

That first time it happened, Marcella thought Benny Boo must be a little strange, worrying about the police all the time and walking off to watch TV with not so much as a "good-bye, see-you-later." But then she got used to the fact that Benny Boo watched reruns of "Mr. Ed" every day at four o'clock, no matter what else happened. She learned not to smile too much and never to mention the police.

In return, Benny Boo showed her his workbench, where he sat in the garage while he carved hunks of wood into small replicas of the Statue of Liberty, which he sold to a gift shop in New York.

Benny Boo had carved one thousand and thirty-three miniatures of the Statue of Liberty. Marcella thought he might be sick and tired of the Statue of Liberty after that, so she once brought him a book from the school library that had other national monuments in it that Benny Boo might be interested in carving.

Benny Boo had glanced through the book, but he went right back to carving the Statue of Liberty, even when Marcella showed him a picture of the White House and told him all about the President living there!

Marcella gave up on the White House. Instead, she impressed Benny Boo by collecting empty aluminum cans from Judge Willa Scott's trash.

Judge Scott was an elderly retired judge who lived five blocks from Benny. She didn't drink much soda pop. But if Benny spied any empty cans in her trash, he would whimper and fret and wring his hands at the sight of those lost aluminum cans.

Marcella promised Benny she'd get the cans for him. Benny Boo was too afraid to ask Judge Scott for the cans because he reasoned a judge — even a retired one — was the closest thing to the police.

Later, though, Marcella was a little sorry she had made that promise because sometimes she didn't have time to get the cans after school before she stopped at Benny Boo's garage, which always made him fret needlessly.

Since she hadn't had a chance to get Judge Scott's cans today, she expected Benny Boo would whine about them. When she opened the door to the workshop-garage, stepped in, and Benny Boo looked up soulfully at her from his workbench, she knew something must be terribly wrong. He didn't say one word about the cans!

"Aren't you going to ask me about Judge Scott's cans, Benny?"

"Nope."

Marcella tried again. "Aren't you going to ask me who's been chasing me?"

Marcella figured that question would shake Benny Boo into asking her if the police had been chasing her.

"Nope."

"Why not?"

"Because I got a letter today."

Marcella couldn't understand why getting a letter would have anything to do with him not being interested in Judge Scott's cans or somebody chasing her. But she did know that getting a letter must be a big concern to Benny Boo. Benny Boo never got letters. Still, she didn't understand why he was depressed about it. When *she* got letters, they were almost always from her grandmothers, and they often included money!

"Did you get any money in it?" Marcella asked, hoping he had. But she supposed if he'd gotten money, he would have told her about it.

15

"I haven't even opened it," Benny Boo said, picking up the envelope from the corner of his workbench and pressing it back down in its spot again. "But I know it's from my brother. James. See." He pointed to the letters on the return address. "J-A-M-E-S. James. I can't read anything else," he admitted. "Before my daddy died, my daddy used to read James's letters. But then he got so he couldn't see, so our neighbor Mrs. Jacobs read them for us. Then James used to call me on the telephone, but now he's writing me letters again."

Marcella looked puzzled. "If James knows you can't read letters, why didn't he call you on the telephone this time?"

"I don't answer it anymore."

Marcella frowned. "Why don't you answer it?"

Benny Boo looked at Marcella funny, as if she must be really dumb not to figure it out. "Because I know it's James calling. He won't quit calling until I come live with him. He says I can't live here any longer by myself. On account of I'm retarded and our daddy's dead. Mrs. Jacobs checks up on me every day. And I get food three times a day from a restaurant. James asks them to bring it. But James says it's not enough. He wants me to come live with him."

"But you don't know for sure that's what James wants," Marcella reasoned. "Why don't you open the letter? Maybe James is only coming for a visit."

Benny Boo wrapped his thick arms around his head and shook himself. "No — oo! I don't want him to come for a visit. He'll take me to live with him. I don't want to leave my home."

Marcella had never seen Benny Boo so upset. She didn't know what to do. She decided to change the subject. "You want me to go get Judge Scott's cans now, Benny?"

He lowered his arms. "No." He picked up the letter and handed it to Marcella, its edge between his finger and thumb, as if it were something distasteful. "I want *you* to read the letter."

Marcella took the letter, tore it open, and unfolded the sheet of paper. The letter was really short, but it was written in cursive, and Marcella had trouble reading other people's cursive. She picked out enough of the words to understand that the letter was from James and that James was coming to get Benny Boo in two weeks to come live with him in Washington, D.C.

But when Marcella glanced up from reading the letter, she knew by the hopeful look on Benny Boo's

17

face that she couldn't tell him that. She had to think of something that wouldn't upset him. Fast.

"He wants to know," Marcella began. "He wants to know if you want a dog."

Marcella didn't know where that idea came from, except she'd been thinking about the missing Riverview dog. She couldn't see what harm changing the letter would do, though. If Benny Boo had wanted a dog, he would have had one by now, she reasoned. So Benny Boo would say no, he didn't want a dog. At least *her* version of the letter didn't make Benny Boo hold his head and moan.

"It's some kind of a trick," Benny Boo said, rubbing the back of his neck. "James never let me have a dog before. He pays all my bills." Suddenly, a spark of understanding lit Benny Boo's face. "He's going to give me a dog if I come live with him. But I'm too smart for him. I'll get my own dog."

Marcella knitted her brows, not understanding what Benny Boo meant, except that he might be leaving. She didn't want Benny to leave. "Can your brother really do that? Can he make you come live with him?"

Benny Boo didn't answer her question. All he said was, "Uh-oh. It's four o'clock." Then he disappeared, leaving Marcella holding his letter.

* * *

Marcella always got this jittery feeling in the pit of her stomach when she approached Judge Willa Scott's house. It was a big house with droopy, eye-like dormers up high. The dormers always made the house look as if it were on the verge of flinging its eyes wide open, popping open its mouth of a door and swallowing Marcella up.

The south greenhouse addition was where Marcella always picked out Benny Boo's cans from the trash barrel. It was also where Judge Scott spent most of her time, which made it difficult for Marcella to take the cans without being detected.

Lately, though, Marcella had been finding the cans already sorted into a paper bag and waiting for her to retrieve them from a spot near the greenhouse door. Whenever Marcella sneaked them away, she pretended Judge Scott was a wicked old witch who cast spells on anyone who came near her house. The witch, according to Marcella's game, turned people into empty soda-pop cans. It was Marcella's secret mission to free those poor souls from the witch's magic. That or be turned into a soda-pop can herself!

Usually, Marcella would wait to make sure Judge Scott was not hobbling around in the greenhouse, then run to its exterior door, snatch up the paper sack of cans, and run away. She checked every day for the cans, even though there were usually only one or two. But apparently Judge Scott had been watching Marcella pick up the cans because when she reached for the bag, the greenhouse door flew open and Judge Scott said in a sharp voice, "You're late!"

Marcella froze, slowly daring to glance up at the frail bird of a woman, whose beaklike, pocked nose hung down near her wrinkled mouth and whose piercing eyes demanded an explanation.

"I had homework," Marcella stammered.

"Overruled!" Judge Scott swung the door wider. "Come in before I hold you in contempt."

Marcella reluctantly stepped into the greenhouse.

"There's the garden hose over there." Judge Scott pointed her cane at a green coil beneath a table of potted plants. "Set the nozzle on a fine spray and water everything. Except for Sampson and Kurt," she said, pointing to an aloe and a cactus.

Marcella thought Judge Scott was a pretty nervy cactus herself, demanding instead of asking that Marcella water her plants.

The whole experience wasn't all that bad, though. Marcella enjoyed spraying the water over the two long tables of plants. The only bad part was Judge Scott hovering over her, yelping out directions.

"Not so much on Herbert! He'll drown."

Herbert was a geranium. Marcella didn't think Herbert would drown, but she did think it was odd that all of Judge Scott's plants were boys. There was Elwood, the philodendron; Addison, an African violet; and Maurice, an asparagus fern. Marcella only knew those names because Judge Scott called to the plants as Marcella watered. "Don't feel sorry for yourself, Elwood! Rise up from your roots and shake out of this stagnation!"

Marcella felt itchy until she mustered enough courage to ask the question, "Why have you named all the plants with boy names?"

"Did I give permission for interrogatives?"

Marcella shook her head.

"I've decided to answer that question after all," Judge Scott suddenly said. "All my plants have strong sturdy names. I'm going to die soon, and they're going to need strong names to carry on."

Marcella made a big mistake. Maybe not so much because she thought Judge Scott's explanation was

21

silly, but because she needed something to break the tension in the greenhouse. She laughed.

"Order!" Judge Scott shrieked. She tapped her cane straight down several times on the cement floor. "You think I'm making that up, don't you? The part about dying? You think it's a figment of my imagination."

Marcella didn't know whether to nod or shake her head. Either might set Judge Scott off again. "What's a figment?" she asked instead.

Judge Scott stiffened. "And you say you were late from doing your homework? What's your name, little girl?"

"Wel-l," Marcella began. "Maybe that wasn't true. The part about doing my homework."

"A-ha! I knew it! Gentlemen, there's a perjurer in our midst."

"What's a perjurer?"

"A perjurer is someone who doesn't tell the Truth, the whole Truth, and nothing but the Truth."

Marcella felt naked. "I have to go now," she muttered, re-coiling the hose to its former position.

"You've forgotten something," Judge Scott said, tapping her cane along behind Marcella to the door.

"Oh, my name. My name is Marcella Star-buckle."

Judge Scott shook her head.

"Oh, the cans," Marcella said, stepping outside and picking up the paper bag.

"No, no, no," Judge Scott clucked, shaking her head. "You have forgotten the definition of fig-ment." She cleared her throat. "A figment is a lie based on the truth."

Marcella blinked back at her. "You mean like a dream?"

"Sustained." Then Judge Scott said something stranger than anything else. "You may come again tomorrow. We only have two weeks until I die."

Marcella ran all the way home, something more troublesome than the Fantastic Four hot on her heels.

4

Marcella rattled and shook and twisted the front doorknob of her house. The door wouldn't budge. She'd forgotten her key! What else could go wrong? Benny Boo might move away from Riverview, Judge Willa Scott was dying in two weeks, she had a note from her teacher, and the Fantastic Four thought she was a red herring.

To top all that off, why couldn't she be like lots of other kids with mothers who weren't business mothers and were at home to unlock the door? And it wasn't only that she needed someone to unlock the door. She needed someone to talk to.

"It won't open without a key," a voice said from behind her.

Marcella swung around so quickly that the storm door hit her in the knee. "Ouch! Who said that?"

She didn't see anybody anywhere. Added to everything else that happened that day, was she now hearing things? Was she going crazy?

"I said it."

Marcella looked down at the sidewalk in front of her house. There was no one there! No one but a scruffy-looking dog.

Naw. It couldn't be, Marcella thought to herself. Dogs don't talk. Especially dogs with no pedigree. Which was what this dog was — a mongrel, a stray, a mousy-colored shaggy dog with some black and white spots that sort of ran into each other. He *did* look rather intelligent in the eyes, though. His eyes showed more white around the edges than most dogs Marcella had seen. Still, dogs don't talk. She told him so.

"Okay," he said. "Dogs don't talk. But if you don't mind a dog giving you some advice, you might look under the welcome mat for a spare key."

Marcella rattled and shook and twisted the knob harder. The dog was a figment, she told herself. A figment of her imagination, like Judge Willa Scott said. He might be a real dog, but he was talking only because Marcella wanted somebody to talk to her, to tell her what to do. She kicked back the welcome mat in front of the door. A spare key was there!

"Thanks." Marcella picked up the key and turned it in the lock. She knew she didn't have to thank the dog, because the dog had never really talked to her. But she was so glad to have the door open, she felt generous. She slipped inside the screen door and locked it behind her. She thought that would be the end of her figment, but the dog loped up onto the porch and talked to her through the screen.

"Say, I'm awfully hungry."

"You can have a cookie," Marcella told the dog.

"Chocolate chip?"

Marcella nodded. Of course, her figment *would* know the cookies in the kitchen cupboard were chocolate chip.

"Wait here. I'll get you one."

Marcella flung down her notebook and schoolbooks and the paper bag with Benny's cans in it on the living-room sofa. She skipped to the kitchen and fished out the chocolate chip cookies from the cupboard. She took one for herself and one for the figment. When she slipped it through a crack in the screen door, the dog wolfed it down before she got the door locked again.

"Could I come in?" the dog asked. "I hate to eat alone."

"But you've already eaten. Your cookie is gone."

"I was going to ask for another."

Marcella munched on the edge of her own cookie. "I can't let you in the house. My mother is allergic to dogs. That's why we don't have a dog of our own."

The dog waited a minute, then he said, "That's what she tells you. She's not really allergic to dogs. She just doesn't want you to have one."

"Are you calling my mother a liar?"

"I would never do that. I would never call you a liar either. I'm calling for another cookie."

Marcella let the dog in. But before she could get them each another cookie, the figment raced up the stairs and dashed in and out of the second-floor bedrooms. Then everything got quiet.

Marcella ran up the stairs after the figment. "Figment," she called. "Come out of hiding, Figment. You can't stay up here. My mother will find you." She looked and looked for Figment in all the bedrooms. She found him wedged under her bed, his eyes shining out at her like two black crystal balls.

"If you let me stay the night, I'll help you with

your homework," Figment said in a muffled voice from beneath the bed.

"What does a dog know about homework?"

"Lots of things. I grew up watching 'Jeopardy' on TV. I can question you an answer on anything."

"Okay, then," Marcella said, thinking of her favorite subject. "The President lives here."

"What is the White House?"

"Amazing."

"I can do lots of stuff," Figment pointed out, still trying to impress her. "I can answer the telephone. I can vacuum rugs. I can dust."

That's when Marcella heard the back door slam downstairs and her mother call out to her. "Can you pretend you're not even here?" Marcella said to the dog.

"I can pretend *you're* not even here."

Marcella walked slowly down the stairs to where her mother had collapsed onto the sofa in the living room.

"There you are, Marcella. What were you doing?"

"My homework."

"Good for you. What do you want for dinner?"

Marcella pretended to think about it. Actually,

Marcella was waiting for something to happen before she answered. She was waiting for her mother to start sneezing, or to break out in a rash, or for big welts to pop up all over her arms, which is what Mrs. Starbuckle had said would happen if she came close to where a dog had been.

Nothing happened. Marcella kept waiting for something to happen, but it never did.

"I want red herring for dinner."

"Red herring?" Her mother looked at her funny. "Wherever did you get a crazy notion like that? Are you feeling all right?"

"No. I may have to stay home from school tomorrow. Too bad, too, since I already did my homework."

Mrs. Starbuckle said slowly, "Honey, we don't have any fish in the house. But I can order in your favorite pizza." Mrs. Starbuckle's eyes got bigger as she tried to persuade Marcella with her face.

"No pizza," Marcella heard Figment whisper from upstairs. "Fish or steak or fried chicken."

Marcella repeated Figment's words to her mother.

"All right," her mother said, boosting herself up off the sofa. "I'll go see what I can find in the refrigerator. But you're not acting like yourself, Marcella."

"Neither are you." But her mother didn't hear her. If her mother really were allergic to dogs, she would have sneezed at least once by now.

For dinner that night, Marcella had four pieces of fried chicken, three rolls with butter and jelly, and two big helpings of mashed potatoes with extra gravy. She ate from a tray in her bed. Afterward, her mother took her temperature. It read normal. Her mother said she would see how Marcella was feeling in the morning.

For breakfast in bed the next morning, Marcella asked for four pieces of toast and two helpings of scrambled eggs. After that, she said, "Pancakes, please."

It wasn't often that Marcella could get this much attention from her mother at breakfast. Usually, both her parents were up early and left for work before Marcella fixed herself a bowl of cereal, which she ate alone. But because Marcella had sneaked so much of the food she pretended to eat

31

to Figment the night before, her mother hadn't left early for work this morning. She had stayed to fix breakfast for Marcella and to hover over her when Marcella asked for so much to eat again.

Marcella's mother filled Marcella's plate twice with two heaping stacks of big fat hotcakes. "Wherever are you putting all this food? You must have a tapeworm!"

"What's a tapeworm?"

"Never mind," Marcella's mother said, her eyes wide with fright. "I'm calling the doctor to get you an appointment."

But when she returned from making the phone call, she explained to Marcella that the doctor couldn't see Marcella until tomorrow, tapeworm or no tapeworm. "I hate to leave you here alone all day, Marcella."

"Oh, that's okay. I'm not alone."

"Oh?" her mother said, quizzically.

"The tapeworm," Marcella said, thinking of Figment, stuffed full of Marcella's breakfast under the bed.

Marcella's mother hiccuped and left for work.

"You'd better tell her you didn't eat all that food by yourself," Figment said when Marcella's mother had left. "You don't want to go to the doctor, do you?"

"I don't mind. My mother goes with me and everyone is always concerned about what's wrong with me. Then there's Doctor Bingham. He's nice. He always talks to me a lot. I like going to the doctor. I'm the center of attention."

"Well, then, you'd better not do your homework after all. Everybody will think you're sick for sure."

"But you promised to help me with it. I like doing homework if somebody does it with me."

She pulled out her science book and took out a fresh sheet of paper. "I'm supposed to draw the parts of a flower," Marcella explained. "What's your favorite flower, Figment?"

"Dogwood."

Marcella and Figment got along splendidly until late in the afternoon after they had finished all of Marcella's homework, watched "Jeopardy" on television, and played five games of Clue. Marcella dressed as if she had gone to school. She wanted to go see Benny Boo. She asked Figment if he wanted to go with her.

"I'd better not."

"Why?"

"Because you might not let me back in the house again."

"I'll let you back in the house again, Figment." Marcella proved it to him by standing at the back door and holding the screen open while he dashed out of the house, ran willy-nilly around the backyard, and back into the house. Three times!

"See?"

"Well, just the same," Figment said, sitting on the back porch and peeking out the screen at her when she closed the door, "I'd better stay here and answer the phone if anyone calls."

Marcella shrugged. "Okay. If that's what you want to do." She left Figment peering out at her from behind the screen. Even though he'd said he wanted to stay home, Marcella sensed that Figment still didn't believe that if he went with her to Benny Boo's she would let him back in the house.

Maybe it was just as well that Figment hadn't come with her, Marcella decided, as she fingered Benny Boo's letter from his brother, James, deep down in her pocket. Somehow, Marcella was going to have to figure out a way to tell Benny Boo that his brother was coming to Riverview to take him away. If Figment were along, he might say the wrong thing when she was trying to explain why she'd lied.

And Marcella didn't know yet how she was going to tell Benny Boo the truth. Maybe she could tell him she got the words of James's letter all mixed up. Benny Boo couldn't expect her to be a perfect reader, could he?

Maybe she could tell him she needed glasses. *That* was why she hadn't been able to read the letter right. She could tell him she was going to the doctor tomorrow. That wasn't a lie.

Or maybe she wouldn't tell Benny Boo anything about the letter at all. Maybe she would tell him about Figment instead. Maybe she would tell Benny Boo that Figment might be the missing Riverview dog, and she was the only one in the whole town who knew where he was. Except now Benny Boo would know, too, and wasn't it fun to know something nobody else knew?

No, she couldn't do that. Marcella knew Figment was not the missing Riverview dog. Figment didn't look like the picture of the dog that Mrs. Crandall had shown Marcella's class at school. But she knew he was just as special. Figment could talk.

As it turned out, though, Marcella didn't have the chance to tell Benny Boo anything. When she knocked on the door of Benny Boo's workshop-garage, he wouldn't open the door. "Go away!" he yelled at her from inside.

"Benny, it's Marcella. I've brought Judge Scott's cans." She even rattled them in the paper bag to prove it.

"Go away and leave me alone. You're like all the rest. You lied to me. My brother called me on the telephone."

Marcella sank against the door. "Why did you answer the phone, Benny?"

"Because I knew it was James." Benny Boo paused. Then: "You lied to me. He doesn't want to give me a dog. He wants to take me away from here."

"But I didn't want you to go," Marcella whimpered at the door. "And I didn't want to scare you. I couldn't think of anything else to say."

"Go away," Benny Boo repeated. "Go away, go away, go away."

Marcella set the bag with Judge Scott's cans in it at the bottom of Benny Boo's door. Then she walked away with tears streaming down her face. She wondered if Benny Boo were crying, too.

But at least he wouldn't be alone if he went to live with his brother, James. Marcella had been alone lots of times. Especially before she met Benny Boo. He just couldn't move away. He just couldn't!

Marcella chose the wrong time to step out into
Benny Boo's alley. Before she could jump back behind the workshop-garage, the Fantastic Four
lunged at her.

"There she is!" Tammy Collins screamed.
"What did I tell you? I knew I saw Marcella sneak-
ing around here!"

Marcella would have run away, but the four of
them crowded around her.

"Why weren't you in school today, Marcella?"
Libby Grimes asked. "I brought the birthday invitation, but you weren't there." Libby pulled out a
folded card that had brightly colored balloons and
confetti on the front of it. Marcella wanted that
invitation more than anything in the world. But
Libby didn't hand it to Marcella. Libby tucked it
back inside her notebook.

"She wasn't in school," Tammy Collins said, rocking back and forth on her heels, "because she didn't want to tell where the dog is. She wants to keep all the reward money for herself."

"We followed you here, Marcella," Linda Cappanelli said. "So now we know where the dog is."

"The Retard has him!" Jill Kramer clapped her hands and jumped up and down.

"Benny's not a retard!" Marcella shouted. "Don't call him that. He hates to be called that."

"Oh, yeah?" Tammy Collins crooned, planting her hands at her hips. "Retard. Retard. Retard. We can call him anything we like. Unless you think you can stop us." Tammy's chin stuck out and her eyes darkened.

Marcella didn't think she could stop Tammy and the other members of the Fantastic Four from calling Benny Boo names, but she just might be able to lead them away from him.

"Look," she said, pulling Benny's letter from James out of her pocket and dangling it in front of them. "I only came here to give Benny back his letter. He wanted me to read it for him."

"Pee-uuu. I wouldn't even touch something that belonged to The Retard," Jill Kramer squealed. She scrunched up her perky little nose so it looked as dried up and wrinkled as Judge Willa Scott's nose. That gave Marcella an idea of how to get the Fantastic Four away from Benny Boo.

"Well, it doesn't matter anyway," she said. "Because Benny's not home. But if you want to know where the dog really is, come with me." Marcella started walking off down the alley, but the Fantastic Four didn't follow her.

"Where are you going?" Libby Grimes asked.

"To Judge Willa Scott's house."

"No way!" Tammy Collins exclaimed. "Judge Willa Scott is crazy. Everybody says so. I'm not going anywhere near her."

"Suit yourself," Marcella said, shrugging. She walked on alone, glancing back over her shoulder every five steps (five was Marcella's favorite number). The Fantastic Four must have decided to split up, because after a lot of whining and yelling at each other, Marcella caught sight of Libby Grimes and Jill Kramer following her. Tammy Collins and Linda Cappanelli stayed at Benny Boo's garage.

Marcella knocked on the back door of Judge Willa Scott's greenhouse. The door flew open and Judge Willa Scott stood there. "What do you want?"

"You asked me to come again today. To water your plants."

"I did not!"

"You did," Marcella insisted.

"Not to water the plants. Do you want them to drown?"

Marcella didn't want the plants to do anything. She wanted Libby Grimes and Jill Kramer to quit following her. Judge Willa Scott was the perfect person to scare them away.

"Who are those girls in the alley?" Judge Scott asked Marcella. "Friends of yours?"

"Not exactly. I know them from school, but they're not exactly friends."

"Well, what are they then?" Judge Scott squinted her eyes and studied Libby and Jill.

"They're curious," Marcella explained. "About you."

"Ah-ha!" Judge Scott snorted so abruptly that Marcella jumped. "Thrill seekers!" She snorted again and then said to Marcella in a lower voice, "Should I roll my eyes and flap my arms?"

Marcella laughed. "I don't think so. They're already pretty scared of you."

"Hummph. Ask them to come in, then. That should do the trick."

Marcella walked back out to the alley to where Jill and Libby were standing. "Judge Scott asked me to ask you if you want to come in."

"No way!" Jill said. "She's a witch! She turns people into plants."

Libby rolled her eyes. "Who, for instance? Nobody but a dog is missing from Riverview."

"Well ... well ... I don't know. It's what I heard," Jill said.

A spark lit Libby's face. "Let's go in and find out for sure," she said.

"And get turned into a plant?" Jill's eyes doubled in size. "I don't know why I came here in the first place. I'm getting out of here!"

Jill sped away down the alley. Marcella looked at Libby and shrugged. Then Marcella turned back to the greenhouse and opened the door.

"Hey, wait a minute, I'm coming with you," Libby called. "I don't believe in witches."

"Okay, but don't ask too many questions. Judge Scott does all the asking."

"What's taking you so long?" Judge Scott asked, tapping her cane. "You have work to do!"

"Work?" Libby looked puzzled. "What work?"

"Well, you didn't come here to watch me die, did you?"

"I came to ask you about the missing Riverview dog."

Uh-oh. Libby was in big trouble now.

"If I want questions, *I'll* ask them," Judge Scott roared.

"See. Here." Libby pulled a newspaper clipping from her notebook. It was the clipping that Mrs. Crandall had read to the fourth-grade class.

Judge Scott snatched the clipping from Libby's hand. "Hummph. Newspapers! I never read them. They're full of bad news. Who needs bad news when dying is bad enough?"

"You're dying?" Libby asked and then glanced at Marcella with a strange look on her face.

"In thirteen days," Judge Scott announced proudly. "Which reminds me," she said, tucking the newspaper clipping into the pocket of her gardening smock. "Before I die, all the plants have to be repotted. And Rasputin has to be fed."

"Who's Rasputin?" Marcella asked.

"Rasputin is my Venus's-flytrap. I've had him for ten years. He was a gift from a dear friend when I retired from the bench."

"Did he used to be a person?" Marcella asked, trying to get to the truth about Jill's Judge-Scott-turning-people-into-plants story.

"My dear girl!" Judge Scott exclaimed. "You've been watching too much television! Try doing your homework for a change."

Marcella announced proudly, "I did my homework today."

"Marcella, you never do your homework," Libby moaned. "She's lying," she told Judge Scott.

"Overruled!" Judge Scott barked at Libby. "Never make an objection without sufficient proof. Hearsay is not good enough. Both of you could use a lesson or two in evidence. But botany will have to do. That's the study of plants."

"We're studying plants in school," Marcella said. "In science."

Judge Scott looked at Libby, as if she expected an objection. "It's true," Libby said. "The parts of the flower."

"Well, then, we won't feed Rasputin today. Not until you've done your homework on the Venus's-flytrap."

"Oh, please," Libby begged. "I've never seen a Venus's-flytrap eat something before."

"Overruled. Not until you're prepared. We'll do that tomorrow."

"I can't tomorrow," Marcella said. "My mother's

44

taking me to the doctor. I may have a tape-worm."

"A tapeworm?" Judge Scott looked at Marcella. "What you have, my dear, is an overactive imagination."

"Yeah," Libby agreed. "She's always telling wild stories that nobody believes."

Marcella plunked down the clay pot Judge Willa Scott had handed her. "For your information, some of them happen to be true!"

"Aha!" Judge Scott snorted. "It's not always easy to separate fact from fiction. But separate you must!" She fished into her gardening smock for the newspaper clipping and handed it back to Libby. "Adjourned. Adjourned. We're adjourned." She waved Marcella and Libby out the greenhouse door. "Go ask around town. See if anyone knows anything about that dog."

"But we're not finished," Libby argued.

"You're finished. And so am I in thirteen days. Go find anyone who knows anything about that dog."

Marcella and Libby stumbled out the green-house door. "What got into her?" Libby thought out loud. "One minute we're potting plants, the

45

next minute she wants us hunting for the missing Riverview dog."

Marcella shrugged. "I suppose that's the way somebody who's going to die acts."

"You believe that? That she's going to die in thirteen days?"

Marcella shrugged again. "It's hard to tell."

"Well, I don't. I think she's scared. Scared because we know about the dog and she knows something, too. Something she doesn't want to tell us. We have to go back and find out what she knows."

If Judge Scott was scared, she wasn't the only one, Marcella thought to herself. Marcella was scared about Figment. She was scared that she might not be able to keep Figment a secret from her parents.

"I don't want to go back to Judge Scott's," Marcella said.

"Not now. In a couple of days," Libby suggested.

"Are you going to tell Jill and Tammy and Linda what Judge Scott said about looking for the dog?"

"I'll have to tell them something," Libby reasoned.

"Tell them Judge Scott is dying in thirteen days, and she's coming back as a Venus's-flytrap."

Libby laughed. "If I told them that, they'd probably believe it."

"It would serve them right for being mean to Benny."

Libby slowly shook her head. "You sure have strange friends, Marcella. And you make up even stranger stories." Marcella hung her head. "But you're a lot of fun." That lifted Marcella's head a little higher. "Except one of these days, your stories are going to get you in big trouble."

Maybe so, Marcella thought to herself. But so far her stories had gotten her people to talk to.

7

"Where have you been, young lady?"

Marcella's mother glared at Marcella. Her hands were folded firmly across her chest. She was starting to bite at her lower lip, something Mrs. Starbuckle did whenever she was upset.

Uh-oh, Marcella thought. Her mother was really angry. Had she found Figment and started sneezing? No sign of Kleenex anywhere. No sign of Figment either.

If it weren't for Figment, Marcella would enjoy her mother's anger. The house didn't seem so lonely. It seemed full of her mother's voice and Marcella's feelings.

"Do you realize I've been on the phone ever since I got home?" Mrs. Starbuckle asked.

Good, Marcella thought. Then maybe her mother hadn't had time to discover Figment.

"I've called everyone I could think of, asking where you were. I even called Mrs. Crandall to see if you'd decided to go to school today. She had a lot of things to tell me even though she didn't know where you were."

"And I've got a lot of things to show you!" a voice coming in the back door behind a mountain of packages said.

"Daddy!"

Marcella leaped into the outstretched arms of her father even before he could drop the packages. "I'm so glad you're home! Can we play I-Spy tonight? Can we pop popcorn together and catch it in our mouths? Can we keep score and the loser has to listen to everything the winner did today? Can we? Can we?"

Mr. Starbuckle's face drooped. "I'm sorry, Baby-cakes. But your old man has to take his nose back to the grindstone tonight. I only stopped in to bring you these things from my trip to Chicago."

Marcella's eyes dropped to the floor.

"Wait'll you see!" He popped a Barbie doll out of a package. Then he proudly displayed two other dolls next to Barbie. His face lit up as he pulled a brown wrapper off the biggest package of all. It was a Barbie-sized camping trailer, complete with campfire and stools and a tent on the trailer that expanded or collapsed at Barbie's whim. Mr. Starbuckle's eyes were wide with expectation at Marcella's reaction.

"Nice, daddy. Thanks. But you already brought me these dolls from San Francisco. And the camping trailer from Houston. Don't you remember?"

"Wait a minute, Brad," Mrs. Starbuckle said. "I'm the one who has to work tonight. Don't you remember me telling you that I'm taking Marcella to the doctor tomorrow? If I take off early for that tomorrow, I've absolutely positively got to work tonight. Unless *you* can take Marcella to the doctor tomorrow?"

"Me? Honey, I have a big meeting tomorrow. What's wrong with Marcella?"

"I have a tapeworm," Marcella boasted. "It's eating away at my insides. It's eating a hole in my stomach, and next it's going to eat all my funny bones."

Mr. Starbuckle rumpled Marcella's hair. "Cute kid. Tapeworms. Gee. Where do you get such ideas?"

"Well, it's not from homework," Mrs. Starbuckle said. "I talked with Mrs. Crandall today. She said Marcella hasn't done her homework in days. She said Marcella is a child crying out for help."

"Are you crying out for help?" Mr. Starbuckle asked Marcella, a sappy grin on his face as he made fun of the idea.

"It's not funny, Brad. Mrs. Crandall says that Marcella tells all kinds of wild stories to her and the other kids. She has imaginary friends and made-up pets that eat her homework. She has no friends because no one wants to be friends with a liar."

"That's not true!" Marcella cried. "I do too have friends. Libby Grimes is my friend. She's a detective. She's hot on the trail of the missing Riverview dog. And I'm her partner."

"Got any leads?" Marcella's father said, playing along with Marcella.

"At first we did. But now we think she might be a red herring," Marcella said, beaming with pride at her use of the recently learned expression. "Judge Willa Scott."

"You stay away from that woman," Mrs. Starbuckle said. "She's crazy. Everybody says so."

"She is not crazy," Mr. Starbuckle argued. "A little senile, maybe, but not crazy."

"What's senile?" Marcella asked, but neither of her parents heard her. If she had been talking with Judge Willa Scott, the elderly woman would have answered her question, even though she liked to ask the questions herself. It occurred to Marcella that Judge Scott was very wise. That is, when she wasn't acting senile, whatever that meant.

"Will you stop worrying about Marcella, Ellen?" Mr. Starbuckle said. "And you start doing your homework, young lady." Mr. Starbuckle said to Marcella.

"I did my homework today," Marcella told him proudly.

"Good girl."

"Figment helped me do it."

"Figment, huh? Gee, some people nowadays come up with the weirdest names for their kids."

"I have to go back to the office," Mrs. Starbuckle interrupted. "Dinner's in the oven. I absolutely positively have to get going."

"Well, what about me?" Mr. Starbuckle wanted to know. "I've got to go, too! And what about Marcella? Who's going to stay with her?"

"Figment can stay with me," Marcella suggested.

"Figment? Oh, Figment," Mr. Starbuckle said as if he suddenly understood. "Ellen, who exactly is Figment?"

"Figment is my best friend," Marcella answered for her mother.

"Figment?" Mrs. Starbuckle said. "I've never heard you mention a Figment in your class. Where's he live?"

"He just moved here."

"And he's coming over to play with you to-night?" Mr. Starbuckle asked.

Marcella nodded. Now nobody could say she didn't have any friends.

"Is that all right with you, Ellen?"

"Wel-l. Ordinarily, I don't like children over unless one of us is at home. But I hate to say no since Marcella never asks to have friends over. It isn't very fair to her."

"Okay, Marcella," her father said. "Here's what we'll do. When Figment gets here, have him call my office number so I'll know he's here." Mr. Starbuckle slipped a business card out of his pocket and handed it to Marcella.

"And have him call my office number a half an

hour later," Mrs. Starbuckle instructed. "Alternate calling your father's number and my number every half hour so we'll know you're all right."

"Okay." After all, Figment said he could answer a phone. Marcella guessed he could place a call as easily as receive one. She imagined Figment could do just about anything. With a little help from her, his best friend.

"Figment! Figment! Come out, come out, wher-ever you are!"

After Marcella's parents left, she looked under her bed for Figment. He wasn't there. She looked under her parents' bed. No luck. She looked under the bed in the guest bedroom. Empty space. She looked in every closet in the house and under all the furniture. Figment had vanished!

Then she heard whimpering. It sounded like someone with a mouth full of socks. She traced the sound to her bedroom. Libby Grimes would have been impressed at Marcella's good detective work.

Then Marcella found Figment. He had stuffed himself inside her Victorian dollhouse!

The dollhouse was huge. It stood nearly as tall as Marcella from where it sat on her bedroom floor. It had been a gift from her father. He brought it back from England when he was gone for two whole months. Now that Marcella thought about it, the dollhouse looked a lot like Judge Willa Scott's house. Except Marcella's dollhouse had eyes peeking out the third-story front windows. Frightened, white-rimmed eyes. And the front door had popped open to make way for a hairy black and white peppered paw and leg.

Marcella ran around to the back of the dollhouse. It was Figment, all right. His head was wedged into the third-story bedrooms, his neck caught in the staircase. His bottom filled the downstairs living room, and his front legs forked into the kitchen and bathroom. Somehow, his tail had been threaded into the living-room fireplace. The tip of it stuck out the top of the chimney on the outside. He was so miserably wedged into the house that he couldn't even talk!

· "Oh, Figment, how on earth did you ever get in there?"

Figment couldn't answer her. His mouth was pried open, his upper teeth hooked onto the third-story staircase rail and his bottom teeth snagged on the second-story banister.

Marcella wondered if she should call the fire

department. The fire department was famous for getting cats out of trees. Surely they could get a dog out of a dollhouse.

But when she went into her parents' bedroom and picked up the telephone receiver, she realized that if she called the fire department, everyone would find Figment. If the fire department came, they might blow their siren and flash their big red light so all the neighbors would rush over to see what was wrong. Then they might see Figment and tell her parents. No, she couldn't call the fire department.

She noticed, too, that it was time for Figment to call her father's office. But how could he? He couldn't even talk!

Marcella dialed her father's office. At first, she thought she would tell her father that Figment's dog got himself caught in her dollhouse and did he have any ideas as to how to get the dog out? But when her father answered, she just couldn't tell him anything.

"Figment speaking," she said into the phone.

"Ah, Figment. Thanks for calling. Is everything all right? You and Marcella okay?"

"We're playing with Marcella's dollhouse."

"Hmm." Her father cleared his throat. "Boys like playing with dollhouses these days, huh?"

"No. I'm trying to get out of it."

"I understand, Figment. Here's an idea. Get the Monopoly game out. Tell Marcella it's more your kind of real estate game."

"Okay. Good-bye, Mr. Starbuckle."

"Figment?"

"Sir?"

"I'm counting on you to keep an eye on Marcella."

"I'll keep two eyes on her, sir."

Then Marcella hung up and ran back to her bedroom, where Figment was whining loudly. She had to do something! Already Figment's mouth was getting all dried out from being wedged open. He was breathing kind of funny, too. Every time he huffed, a blanket from one of the beds in the dollhouse bedroom stuck to his nose.

Marcella reached her hand inside the dollhouse and pulled the blanket off Figment's nose. Somehow, she had to get the roof off the house. If she could get the roof off the house, then the walls on the third floor could be pulled straight up and out. She knew because she had watched her father put the house together. She tried to remember exactly how he had done it. Her father wasn't as easy to watch do something as Benny Boo. Benny Boo always let her get her face down close to the Statue of Liberty when he was carving it.

Benny Boo! Why hadn't she thought of Benny Boo!

Because he probably wouldn't answer his telephone. He wouldn't even speak to her. He hated her now. But if he knew she was in terrible trouble, maybe he would help. He just had to help! Otherwise, poor Figment might suffocate.

Marcella ran to the phone again and dialed Benny Boo's number. She had to look the number up in the phone book first, which took some time, because she'd never called him before.

Marcella could hear the telephone ringing ten times before he picked it up. "James?"

"Benny, this is Marcella. Please don't hang up. I have a big problem and I need your help."

Benny Boo hung up.

Marcella dialed his number again. This time when Benny Boo lifted the receiver — after fifteen rings! — Marcella said really fast, "Benny, there's a dog in my dollhouse and if I don't get him out he's going to suffocate. You have to come over to my house right away. And bring your tools."

"You're making fun of me, Marcella."

"No, Benny. I promise, it's the truth. If you don't help me, I'll have to call the police, and I'm too scared to call the police."

Benny Boo didn't say anything on the other end of the phone. Then he started moaning kind of low. "I don't know, Marcella. You've already tricked me once . . ."

"I promise, Benny," Marcella repeated. "This is not a trick. If you don't hurry, Figment might die, Benny. He's trapped in the dollhouse. He's a dog, Benny. Don't you care about helping a dog?"

Benny Boo paused. "My brother, James, had a dog once. When we were both real little." But it ran away and he never found it.

"That's nice, Benny," Marcella said. "You'll have to tell me about James's dog sometime. Please come over now? Please!"

"All right," he agreed. "I'll come over. With my tools. This better not be a trick."

"It's no trick, Benny. Please hurry!"

After Marcella gave Benny directions to get to her house, she hung up the phone and ran back to Figment to see if he was still breathing. He was, but his eyes were really wide and white, and his nose was drying out real fast since he didn't have a chance to lick it.

Marcella ran downstairs and turned on the front-porch light and the back-porch light so Benny Boo would see where to come. She paced back and forth in the living room since she couldn't stand to look at Figment while she waited. She realized now how much Figment meant to her. If anything happened to him, she would ... she would ... well, she didn't want to think about it.

Finally, there was a knock at the back door. It was Benny Boo! "I never been to your house before," he said, stepping in. "I wasn't sure where to come."

Marcella didn't say hello or anything. "Quick, Benny." She showed him up the stairs to where Figment was wedged inside the dollhouse.

Benny Boo looked at her, more puzzled than usual. "How did he get in there?"

Marcella shrugged. The best she could do to describe why Figment was in the dollhouse was to say, "He thought the police were following him. It was the only place he could find to hide."

"Oh." Benny Boo set to work. He unscrewed the roof from the house and lifted it off. Then, with Marcella giving directions, he pulled the third-story walls up and out of the dollhouse. Then they lifted the third floor out and unwedged Figment's mouth. When Figment was free, he shook his head and did a lot of licking of his nose. He licked Benny Boo's hand, too. Figment tried to wag his tail, but it was still caught in the fireplace. Marcella knew because she could see the chimney move.

"He likes me!" Benny Boo smiled at Marcella. "He really likes me!"

"So do I, Benny," Marcella said, as Benny Boo lifted Figment all the way out of the house and began reassembling the dollhouse. "You've saved Figment and the dollhouse and me. You're a hero!"

"How about that. I'm a hero." Then a puzzled expression passed across Benny's face. "What exactly is a hero?"

With as much wisdom as Judge Willa Scott, Marcella explained, "A hero is somebody who saves somebody else. Someone who is brave and courageous and not afraid of anything."

"I'm not a hero," Benny Boo said, looking up at Marcella from where he knelt on the floor. "I'm afraid of the police. I'm afraid of leaving Riverview. To live with James."

Marcella nodded her head in understanding. "I know, Benny. I'm afraid, too."

9

The next day was the weirdest day Marcella could remember. For starters, her parents didn't rush around getting ready for work. They didn't grab a doughnut from the cupboard and a cup of coffee from the microwave before kissing her quick and whisking out the door to work.

Both Mr. and Mrs. Starbuckle were up early, as if they couldn't sleep very well. Marcella's mother tiptoed into Marcella's bedroom to wake her for school. Marcella's mother almost *never* woke her up for school. Marcella had long ago developed the habit of waking herself. It came from Marcella's knowing that if she wanted to see much of her parents at all, she had to get at least a quick look at them before they left for work in the morning.

It was a good thing that Marcella was already awake and had pushed Figment off her bed and underneath it, or her mother would have found out about him!

"How are you feeling this morning?" Mrs. Starbuckle asked her.

Marcella looked puzzled. She felt about the same as any other morning, except curious as to why her mother would ask. Her mother almost never asked how she felt in the morning.

At breakfast — which was actually a sit-down breakfast with all three of them at the table — Marcella's parents didn't say much. They kept staring at her.

"I can't believe you're hungry," Mrs. Starbuckle finally said.

"I always have a bowl of cereal for breakfast," Marcella explained. She thought maybe her mother wouldn't know that because both her parents had usually gone to work by the time Marcella ate.

"Did you and Figment have a little snack last night?" Mr. Starbuckle wanted to know. "We had to go to the grocery store last night or there would have been nothing for breakfast this morning."

"Oh, well, yes," Marcella stammered. "We did have a little snack."

"A little snack?" Marcella's mother eyed her as

she ate each spoonful of Zippy O's. "A gallon of milk, a dozen eggs, all of the leftover meat loaf, a loaf of bread, and a whole box of chocolate chip cookies."

"Actually, it wasn't a full box of chocolate chip cookies."

Mrs. Starbuckle looked at Mr. Starbuckle. Then they both watched Marcella finish her cereal. "I'll pick you up this afternoon for your doctor's appointment," Mrs. Starbuckle told Marcella.

"I'll take you to school," Mr. Starbuckle said. He brought along a paper bag in case Marcella was sick in the car.

When they reached Riverview Elementary, Mr. Starbuckle parked in the parking lot and walked Marcella to her classroom. After he left, Marcella saw him disappear into the school nurse's office to have a long talk with Miss Addenour. Marcella timed how long her father was in the nurse's office. The genuine Mickey Mouse watch her father had brought her from dumb old California said ten minutes and forty-six seconds! He was definitely late for work.

The second weird thing that happened that day was that Marcella guessed Mrs. Crandall's jewelry wrong. Mrs. Crandall always wore blue on Thursdays. She had worn a blue pantsuit or her blue two-piece dress with blue swirly earrings and matching swirly necklace every Thursday since the beginning of fourth grade. But today she was wearing yellow! A yellow skirt with matching yellow sweater that had yellow ribbons threaded through it.

To top it all off, Mrs. Crandall didn't wear a necklace at all! She wore gold earrings.

"Mrs. Crandall," Marcella gasped. "You have gold earrings."

"Why, yes, Marcella. They're new."

"But you can wear gold earrings with anything," Marcella said nervously. "You can wear them with your green suit or your blue pantsuit or your red dress."

"That's what I thought when I bought them, Marcella. In fact, that's why I bought them."

Then Marcella remembered something. "Sometimes when my mother buys fake gold jewelry, it turns green. Do you suppose yours will do that?"

Mrs. Crandall looked at Marcella funny. Marcella didn't say anything more about the gold earrings.

Now Marcella would never be able to guess Mrs.

Crandall's jewelry. She might never win at her secret game again. In fact, because Mrs. Crandall had changed the game, Marcella didn't think she would play the game ever again. She felt sad about that. She felt funny inside, the same as when her parents watched her eat her cereal at breakfast.

"Marcella played hooky yesterday, Mrs. Crandall."

Marcella looked around to get a better look at Tammy. This was the third weird thing to happen to her that day. She had never known Tammy Collins to snitch on her. Kids in fourth grade would make fun of Marcella for telling tall tales, but none of them ever felt threatened enough by Marcella to tell the teacher. Of course, when Marcella saw that Jill Kramer and Linda Cappanelli were with Tammy, that sort of explained things.

"I know all about that, Tammy," Mrs. Crandall said. "Marcella, you will have to stay inside at recess and make up your work." Then she turned to Tammy. "And you, my dear, need to mind your own business."

Well, that was just about like throwing a glass of cold water on Tammy.

Marcella figured out why Tammy was telling on her. Tammy was afraid the Fantastic Four wouldn't want her as their leader if she didn't do *something* to Marcella. After all, instead of Tammy, it had been Marcella who wasn't afraid of Judge Willa Scott. So Marcella wasn't surprised at the way Tammy was acting.

"Marcella, Marcella, don't-believe-what-she-tells-ya," Tammy chanted to her as she passed by.

"Tammy, Tammy, lost her invitation to my party," a voice mimicked Tammy from behind Marcella.

It was Libby Grimes! And the fourth weird thing that day.

"I'll stay in and help you with your work, Marcella," Libby offered. "If that would be all right with Mrs. Crandall."

Mrs. Crandall beamed. "That's a wonderful idea, Libby."

"And I have another idea," Libby said, standing up tall, shoulders thrown back. "Marcella and I would like to do a special science project on the Venus's-flytrap."

"The Venus's-flytrap," Mrs. Crandall repeated. "What an interesting subject. I'm sure the class would be excited to see a Venus's-flytrap. Do you know of one you can bring to school?"

"Maybe," Libby said, eyeing Marcella. "We'll have to check first."

"That's wonderful, Libby." Mrs. Crandall smiled.

"That's wonderful, Libby." Tammy Collins mocked Mrs. Crandall out of her teacher's hearing in a falsetto voice. "Have you heard the other news?"

"What?" Libby asked.

"The Fantastic Four is now the Terrific Three. You've been canned. Libby, Libby, Libby."

Then Libby did this fantastic thing, which probably proved why she used to be one of the Fantastic Four. She shrugged her shoulders and asked, "Does that mean all three of you won't be coming to my birthday party next week?"

The faces of the Terrific Three wilted.

"Marcella is coming. Aren't you, Marcella?" Libby asked, turning to Marcella.

"Sure," Marcella said, stammering. "As soon as you give me an invitation."

Libby slipped out the invitation from her notebook and handed it to Marcella.

"Silly of me to forget. But you said I might do that. You were right, Marcella."

The Terrific Three were dumbstruck. So was Marcella. Marcella couldn't remember the last time someone said she'd told the truth about something. That was the fifth weird thing that happened to Marcella in one day. And the day wasn't even over yet.

10

"Good news, Marcella," Doctor Bingham said. "There is absolutely nothing wrong with you."

Marcella hugged her arms to her bare chest where she sat naked except for her underwear on Doctor Bingham's examining table. "No tapeworm?" she asked.

"No tapeworm."

Marcella was disappointed. She had hoped to be the only person at Riverview Elementary with a tapeworm. Maybe Doctor Bingham could find something even better wrong with her than having a tapeworm. "What about a brain tumor?"

Doctor Bingham studied Marcella with his opal eyes. Doctor Bingham's eyes were a beautiful blue color. His eyes made up for the fact that the rest of Doctor Bingham looked like Humpty-Dumpty. She wondered if when Doctor Bingham was her age, kids used to call him Egghead. She would have

71

asked him, but Doctor Bingham seemed to want to talk about Marcella instead of himself. That was okay with her.

"Why would you want to have a brain tumor, Marcella?"

"Oh, I wouldn't really want to have one and be sick and everything. But it would be kind of special if I had some disease that wouldn't hurt me or anyone else. You know, something that was really rare that nobody else had."

"Hmm. I see," Doctor Bingham said, as Marcella put her clothes back on.

"Well, I think you do have something that nobody else has."

"Yeah? What?"

"Imaginitis."

"Imaginitis?"

"Yes. It's a very rare disease of the head."

Marcella felt all over her head. Her head didn't feel any different, but if Doctor Bingham said she had a head disease then it must be so. "What exactly are the symptoms?" she asked Doctor Bingham.

"Maybe you'd better tell *me,* since you're the one with the disease, and I'm the doctor."

"Good idea." Marcella sat silent a few moments,

trying to decide whether to tell Doctor Bingham about the strange things that had been happening to her. When she finally decided that Doctor Bingham could be trusted, she asked him a question.

"Do you believe that dogs can talk?"

A smile wiggled over Doctor Bingham's lips, but before it could turn into a full-fledged smile, it melted. "It's strange that you should ask that question, Marcella, because when I was about your age my best friend claimed he had a dog that could talk."

"He did? Did you ever hear the dog talk?"

"No, I didn't believe him. I thought he was saying that about the dog because he wanted to seem special. You see, he had a younger brother who wasn't normal like other kids. That brother got all the attention from my friend's parents. That's why my friend was really close to his dog. He ate, slept, and even talked to his dog. And he said the dog talked back to him."

"But *you* never heard the dog talk?"

"No, I never did." Doctor Bingham sounded sad that he'd never heard the dog talk. "I never got a chance because the dog disappeared. You know how dogs sometimes run away and get lost." Doctor Bingham heaved a big sigh. "The worst part is that my friend was never the same after that. There was a rumor that my friend's father had given the dog away or sold it or some such thing."

Marcella sat very still on the examining table. She was thinking about Figment. About how he talked. And then she was thinking about how terrible she would feel if her parents ever gave Figment away or sold him.

"Do you have a dog that talks, Marcella?"

Marcella looked at Doctor Bingham with a puzzled expression. She didn't know whether to answer yes or no. Figment was a dog, all right, but she couldn't say for sure that he belonged to her. In fact, she was beginning to think that he belonged to someone else, and for the first time, she was thinking about how that other person might feel having lost him. Miserable!

"I don't actually own a dog," Marcella said very carefully.

"But it *was* a dog that ate all that food last night your mother was telling me about," Doctor Bingham guessed.

"Yes."

"And you've managed to keep this dog secret from your mother and father?" Doctor Bingham's eyes lightened in color.

"It hasn't been hard. They aren't home very much." Marcella popped off the examining table. "You won't tell, will you, Doctor Bingham? Not until I figure out what to do with the dog?"

"I think *you* should do the telling, Marcella. And you're going to have to do it soon. Before your parents worry themselves too much about you."

"I will, Doctor Bingham," Marcella promised. "Just as soon as I figure out who the dog belongs to. I'm learning to be a very good detective."

"Detective, huh? Is that what you want to be when you grow up?"

Now Marcella got the feeling Doctor Bingham wasn't believing her anymore.

"No, that's what I want to be right now. Libby Grimes is teaching me how. When I learn to be a good detective, then I'll find out if Figment . . . the dog . . . really talks or not."

Doctor Bingham's face clouded. He picked up a pen and paper from his desk and wrote something on it. "I'm going to give the name of a friend of mine to your mother, Marcella," he said, ripping the paper off its pad. "My friend's name is Doctor Teller. He's a good person to talk to about things such as talking dogs."

"Okay. I like talking to people. Even if sometimes they don't believe me. Like you don't believe I'm working on being a detective, do you, Doctor Bingham?"

"Sure I do, Marcella. But what I really am concerned about is your story about the talking dog."

Marcella smiled. "Well, the two of them sort of go together. Like that friend of yours . . . when you were a kid . . . the one with the talking dog . . . I think I know his name."

"Really, Marcella?" But Doctor Bingham wasn't asking it like he really thought she knew it. He was asking it just to go along with her conversation.

"Yes. His name was James, wasn't it?"

Doctor Bingham looked at Marcella now. He *really* looked at her. His blue eyes blinked with wonder. "That's amazing, Marcella," he finally said. "You're absolutely right. My friend's name was James."

Marcella beamed. It was fun surprising someone with the truth for a change.

Besides feeling good about telling Doctor Bingham
the truth, Marcella felt extra special good when she
found her father with her mother in Doctor Bingham's waiting room. He had left his important
meeting early to come see about her!

Marcella felt like the most special girl in the
fourth-grade class at Riverview Elementary. Correction. She felt like the most special girl in all of
Riverview. Correction. In all of the United States!
No, in all of the world . . . the universe!

She only wished her parents felt the same way.
The little wrinkles that her mother complained
had been showing up around the corners of her
eyes lately were actually showing up. And her father was standing around with his hands in his
pockets, as if he didn't know what to do with himself. Always before, Marcella's father knew what to
do with himself.

The ride home was very quiet. Marcella could tell that there was something important on her mother's mind because she chewed on her bottom lip. Marcella knew that her mother wanted to tell whatever it was to her father by the way Mrs. Starbuckle kept glancing at him.

Marcella wanted to tell her parents what she'd told Doctor Bingham. But she wasn't sure whether or not they could handle the truth about Figment being in the house for three days. And another thing kept her from telling the "whole" truth. Marcella didn't know all of it herself. Had Figment really talked to her? She didn't know. Fine detective she was!

When they were in the car heading home, Marcella's mother glanced at her father while she asked Marcella, "What did you and Doctor Bingham talk about?"

"Well, you know all that food that got eaten last night?" Marcella began.

"Yes," Marcella's parents said together.

"Well, I didn't eat it. A dog ate it."

"A dog? In our house!" Marcella's mother, who was driving since it was her car and Marcella's father had gotten a ride downtown with a friend to Doctor Bingham's, stepped on the brake too quickly, lunging them all forward and then back.

"Isn't it wonderful, Mom? You're not allergic to dogs, after all!"

Marcella's father laughed. "Ellen, is that what you told Marcella? That you're allergic to dogs?"

Mrs. Starbuckle didn't answer him. "What was a dog doing in our house, Marcella? You know I don't like dogs in our house."

"You never said you didn't like them," Marcella said. "You said you were allergic to them. You said that's why I couldn't have one. Because you'd sneeze and puff up and get welts and stuff."

For a minute, the quiet in the car was so eerie that Marcella wanted to scream.

"You haven't answered my question, Marcella," Mrs. Starbuckle said. "What was a dog doing in our house?"

"I bet Figment brought the dog over," Mr. Starbuckle said. "That right, Marcella? It was Figment's dog?"

"Yes," Marcella said. "Figment."

"Well, you can tell Figment, 'No more dogs at our house,'" Mrs. Starbuckle said. Then she suddenly laughed. "Figment's dog must be a bottomless pit. And to think I thought *you* ate all that food." She heaved a big sigh. "It's a relief knowing you didn't. I thought you were developing some terrible eating disorder. Now we can forget about seeing this Doctor Teller. There's nothing wrong with you, Marcella."

"I want to see Doctor Teller." Marcella wanted to see Doctor Teller because first, she liked talking to people, and second, she wanted to ask him about talking dogs. Marcella's parents acted like everything was okay now. The whole family could go back to the way it was before. Marcella didn't want to go back to the way it was before. She couldn't! She didn't know what to do about Figment or Benny leaving or Judge Willa Scott dying or her new friendship with Libby Grimes.

"I thought you had told the truth," Marcella said to her mother. "About being allergic to dogs." Marcella folded her arms across her chest. As soon as the car had stopped in their driveway, Marcella hopped out. "You lied to me!" Marcella slammed the door shut with a big BANG!

Actually, Marcella wasn't all that angry that her mother had lied about being allergic to dogs. She had already known that for three days. She had had time to get used to it. But she thought if she made her parents feel bad about her mother's lie, they might not throw a fit if she had to tell them about

Figment. How Figment was the dog that ate all that food. How Figment had been living in their house for three days. How scared Marcella was that she was going to lose him!

"Hey! Marcella!" her dad called to her. "You aren't being fair. We're trying to help you."

"I don't need help," Marcella blurted out, running into the house, which did no good because her parents ran in after her, and she wanted a chance to go in first by herself to make sure Figment was hidden.

She grabbed a box of crackers off the kitchen counter before dashing upstairs to her room and locking her door behind her. Her parents followed and knocked on her door, asking to come in, but Marcella refused.

"Go away. Go away, go away, go away!"

Finally, they went away.

As soon as it was quiet, Figment came out from under Marcella's bed.

"Am I glad you're home," he said. "I've been waiting for you to get home all day." Figment jumped up on Marcella's bed and dug his nose under her folded arms. "A cracker for your thoughts?"

Marcella opened the box of crackers and gave a

handful to Figment. She watched him wolf them down. She gave him some more. And more and more until the box was empty.

"What am I going to do, Figment? If I tell my parents about you, they're not going to let you stay here."

"Then don't tell them."

Marcella thought silently for a moment. "But now they'll find out. They'll know by how much food is missing." Marcella looked down inside the empty cracker box. Then she looked at Figment, whose big brown eyes begged for more.

"My mother's not going to let me keep you." Marcella stopped. She didn't want to think about losing Figment. Even though she knew it was bound to happen, one way or the other.

"Want to play Monopoly?" Figment asked. "It might take your mind off your troubles for a while."

Marcella threw her arms around Figment. "I love you, Figment. You're the best dog a person could ever have. A game of Monopoly is just the thing I need right now."

Figment said, "Myself, I could use another cracker."

Marcella peered down into the empty box. Then

she looked back at Figment, who, she could tell by the urgency in his eyes, was still hungry. But she couldn't go get more food. Her parents would notice. Still, she wasn't being very fair to Figment, making him wait all day to eat and then not giving him enough. The policeman on one corner segment of the Monopoly game gave Marcella an idea.

"Figment. Maybe you could go stay with Benny for a few days till I think of what to do."

"I like Benny," Figment said.

"Good. And you're so good at giving people ideas, maybe you can get him to quit carving the Statue of Liberty and carve something else."

Figment looked down on Marcella's bed to where the Monopoly game board was spread open. Then he said, "Ever wonder why there are no meat market properties for sale?"

12

The next day at school, there was a note on Marcella's desk. It read: QUIT BEING FRIENDS WITH LIBBY GRIMES OR THE RETARD WILL BE SORRY. IF YOU SHOW ANYONE THIS NOTE, *YOU* WILL BE SORRY. It wasn't signed, but Marcella knew who it was from. Especially when Tammy Collins raised one of her eyebrows when Marcella looked her way.

Marcella slipped the note into her desk. When Libby Grimes smiled at her, Marcella didn't smile back.

"Want to go to Judge Scott's after school today?" Libby whispered to Marcella while retrieving an accidentally-on-purpose dropped pencil.

"I can't," Marcella whispered back. "My parents told me not to go there anymore."

It wasn't a lie. Marcella's mother *had* told her not to go to Judge Scott's. But Marcella did plan to go there. To ask Judge Scott what to do about Figment. But Marcella would have to be very careful. She would have to go *alone*. That meant she would have to say something to Libby to keep Libby away from Judge Scott's.

"Judge Scott died last night," she told Libby.

Libby's face widened with horror. She didn't say one word. In fact, she didn't say anything until science class was over. Finally, she whispered, "Want to go to the library and work on our Venus's-flytrap report?"

Marcella shook her head.

Libby didn't ask Marcella to do anything else together. Libby must have thought Marcella was too sad about Judge Scott dying to do anything. Marcella must have looked sick, too. She felt sick because she was worried her lie about Judge Scott might make the lie come true.

Every recess that day, Marcella stayed in and pretended to work on homework. When Libby offered to stay in with Marcella and help her, Marcella just said, "I'd rather be alone."

Finally, Libby stopped asking to be with Marcella that day. In fact, when no one was looking, Marcella caught a glimpse of Libby on the playground jumping rope with the Terrific Three. Oh well, she told herself, she still had Figment and Benny Boo and Judge Willa Scott. But she knew it was only a matter of time until they would leave her, too.

After school, Marcella slipped out of the classroom before anybody else. She ran to the girls' bathroom and hid there so Libby wouldn't know where she was. When she was sure all of the fourth-grade class had gone home, she ran to Judge Willa Scott's greenhouse.

"What do you want?" Judge Willa Scott said when she answered Marcella's knock.

"I want to know if you're all right."

"Of course I'm not all right. I'm dying in ten days!"

Marcella stepped inside the greenhouse and followed Judge Scott, who hobbled to her rocking chair. "Suppose I could ask you some questions? Since you aren't doing anything until then," Marcella quickly added.

"Who says I'm not doing anything!" Judge Scott roared. "It takes a lot of effort for me just to stay alive ten more days. And why are people always asking me questions?"

Marcella waited a moment for Judge Scott to

calm down. "It's because they think you're wiser than anybody else." She waited until the elderly woman lowered herself shakily into the rocker and began to tap her cane on the floor as she rocked. "Have you ever owned a dog?" Marcella asked.

"Once," Judge Scott said, very softly. Then louder: "But that was a long time ago. And I didn't have the dog for very long. I didn't even really want the dog. What does a woman like me want with a dog? I told the man that. But he was so interested in selling the dog to me, he wasn't thinking about the dog. He needed the money, you see. To pay for a special school for his son." Judge Scott's arms flew up. "Well, of course, when he told me that, it wasn't a question of liking or disliking the dog anymore. I bought the dog so that little boy could go to a special school. I didn't realize . . . I didn't realize . . ."

Tears pooled in Judge Scott's eyes. Marcella crouched close to the rocking chair. She wanted to say something that would make Judge Scott feel better. But she couldn't think of anything. And it made her feel breathless to know that the elderly woman's tears were about to spill down her cheeks.

"So is that all of your questions?" Judge Scott

suddenly thrust herself up and out of the rocker, tapping her cane along the floor, avoiding looking at Marcella.

"No. My real question is kind of complicated. I don't really know how to ask it."

"Well, I only have ten days. If you don't ask me right away, I might run out of time."

Marcella laughed. She thought she saw Judge Scott smile. She supposed that was what made asking Judge Scott about Figment easier.

"Is there really such a thing as a stray dog? A dog nobody owns? A dog that nobody would miss if somebody claimed him?"

"That's enough questions," Judge Scott snapped, suddenly fussing with her plants. She looked intently at Marcella. "Now here's some free advice for you. If you have knowledge of a dog that someone might be missing, you need to place an ad in the newspaper in search of the true owner."

"But I might lose him if I do that," Marcella wailed.

"Better to lose the dog than lose your conscience," Judge Scott said. She stopped to pinch a wilted blossom from Herbert, the geranium.

"What's a conscience?"

"A conscience is a voice inside you that tells you

right from wrong. You never want to lose it," Judge Scott warned, glancing sideways at Marcella. "I lost my conscience once and I've been sorry for thirty years."

Marcella looked wide-eyed at Judge Scott. "Thirty years is a long time to be sorry for losing your conscience."

She paused to think about whether she had a conscience or not. She *did* have a conscience! Figment was always giving her advice, wasn't he?

Well, not always Figment. Marcella glanced out the greenhouse door and heaved a deep sigh. Libby Grimes was standing with hands planted on her hips, scowling at Marcella.

13

"Marcella Starbuckle, you are the biggest liar in the universe!" Libby Grimes shouted. "Judge Scott is not dead. Why did you tell me a big fat lie like that?"

Marcella marched down the alley away from Judge Scott's house. She thought Libby would run away from her. Anyone else would have. Which made Marcella feel rotten, because she knew friends like Libby were not easy to find. Instead of calling her bad names and running away never to speak to her again, Libby stamped behind Marcella, spraying gravel in all directions with every step she took, determined to get at the truth.

"You are the meanest person in fourth grade," Libby continued, kicking at the ground for emphasis. "You are meaner than Billy Cameron when he pulls hair. You are meaner than dumb old Eddie

Wilcox poking everybody with his pencil. You are meaner than Tammy Collins."

Marcella stopped and turned around to face Libby. "I told you that lie so somebody else wouldn't get hurt." Then she trudged on.

"Tammy Collins," Libby cried. "That's it! Tammy Collins had something to do with it! I should have known she would do something like this. She doesn't want us to be friends. How's that for the truth? Pretty good detective work, huh?"

Marcella stopped again. "Look, Libby. I can't be your friend right now, okay? And I can't tell you why. Okay? So please don't ask me any more questions."

Libby sniffed. "I'm not going to ask you any more stupid questions. Don't flatter yourself. I don't have to ask you questions. I'm a detective. I've already got this whole thing figured out. Tammy Collins told you not to be friends with me anymore. I've already figured that out." She stopped to think. Then she ran to catch up with Marcella. "What I don't know is why you agreed. Did Tammy promise you money? Did she promise to do your homework? Did she promise to quit calling you names?"

Marcella ran faster. She was afraid if she stopped, Libby would find out the real reason they couldn't be friends.

"No!" Libby shouted after her. "It's none of those things, Marcella. You don't care about any of those things. It's something worse. Much worse. And I'm going to find out what!"

"Not from me you aren't!" Marcella shouted back.

"Marcella Starbuckle, you are the biggest retard in the universe!" Libby shouted.

This time, they both stopped.

"And I am the best detective in fourth grade," Libby called to Marcella. "It's because of The Retard, isn't it? I knew it. I knew it. I knew it!"

"He has a name," Marcella shouted back. "His name is Benny. No friend of mine calls him Retard."

Libby flashed Marcella a big smile before she ran away.

Darn that Libby Grimes, Marcella thought to herself. Libby was so good a detective it was as if Marcella had blurted out the whole reason they couldn't be friends. Marcella was worried. Libby might be a top-notch detective, but was Libby a good actress? Could Libby pretend she and Marcella weren't friends so Tammy would leave Benny alone?

"Figment! Figment! Where are you, Figment?"

When Marcella got home, she ran upstairs and looked under her bed. Figment was there, wedged between the floor and the bottom of the bed. He scrambled out from underneath it, his large bones thumping against the floor.

Marcella sighed when she saw how Figment had to stretch himself back into shape every time he came out from under her bed. "Figment, we've got to find you a better place to stay." When Figment's peppered brows wormed upward, Marcella quickly added, "It's just until I convince my parents to let me keep you."

Figment yawned from too long a time spent motionless under the bed. "What's for dinner?"

Marcella had brought along another box of crackers. She opened the box and began doling out the crackers to Figment, five at a time, since five was her lucky number. "We've got to find you some better food, too."

"What will I eat for dinner at the new place?"

Marcella hadn't thought of that. Now that she did, it began to worry her. She didn't know what kinds of food Benny ate. All she knew was that a restaurant delivered food to Benny three times a day. She supposed Figment would eat leftovers from Benny's plate. But that might not be enough, either. Marcella had some money her grandmothers had sent her. "I'll buy you some dog food."

"Yuck. I hate dog food! I don't want to go there."

Marcella couldn't blame Figment. She was worried about his going there, too. First of all, Libby Grimes was turning out to be such a good detective that she was bound to find Figment at Benny's. Second, she wasn't sure Benny could take care of Figment. Benny needed taking care of himself!

"Maybe I shouldn't go stay with Benny," Figment said.

"That was exactly what I was thinking." Marcella offered Figment another handful of crackers.

"Does Benny eat dog food?" Figment wanted to know.

"He eats restaurant food."

"He could build me my own bed," Figment said, eyeing Marcella's.

"He could build you a doghouse if you wanted one," Marcella said proudly. "He might even let you watch 'Jeopardy' on television if you ask him nice."

"Are you trying to get rid of me?" Figment said suddenly.

"No, Figment. Honest." Marcella curled her arms around Figment's neck. "No matter what happens, Figment, you will always be my best friend."

"In that case, I'll go to Benny's."

"It'll only be for a few days, Figment. I promise."

Then they heard sudden footsteps on the stairs. Marcella quickly motioned Figment back under the bed. Her bedroom door slowly opened and her mother peeked around it.

"Did I hear voices up here?" Mrs. Starbuckle's eyes scanned the room.

"Just mine, Mom," Marcella said casually. "I was talking to myself."

14

The next day was Saturday, and Marcella's parents always slept late on Saturdays. Today she didn't mind. Today was the day she would take Figment to Benny's. She hadn't asked Benny if Figment could stay with him for a few days, but she was sure Benny wouldn't mind.

Ever since Benny had rescued Figment from Marcella's dollhouse, he seemed like a different person to Marcella. He was a "Benny" instead of a "Benny Boo." Marcella figured Benny's keeping Figment was another chance for Benny to be a hero.

Marcella wished *she* felt like a hero. She knew it was the right thing to do, taking Figment to Benny's, because at Benny's, Figment wouldn't have to hide under a bed all the time and he could eat better food than a box of crackers. But she felt sad about it all the same. Suppose Benny didn't want to give Figment back to her later? Or worse, suppose Figment liked Benny better than her?

"Promise me you won't forget me?" she asked Figment.

"You're unforgettable," Figment told her.

Marcella smiled. She was pleased. But somehow, deep down, she knew that even if she found a way to keep Figment, things were never going to be quite the same in her life again. That's why she took the long route to Benny's. So it would be just her and Figment a little while longer. Figment showed his appreciation for her delaying their parting by wetting on every tree they passed.

Benny was in his workshop-garage. This time when Marcella knocked, he answered the door. "Did you bring Judge Scott's cans?" he asked her first thing. He was his old self again.

"No, Benny. I brought Figment."

Benny watched as Figment ran around the workshop, sniffing at the big pile of cans, sniffing at Benny's workbench, and then whoofing at the refrigerator. "He won't try to get in the refrigerator, will he?" Benny asked.

"No," Marcella said, laughing. "He's usually a very good dog, Benny. That thing with the dollhouse was just an accident."

"I always wanted a dog," Benny confided, watching Figment. "My brother had a dog. He used to like that dog better than me."

"At least you have a brother, Benny. I don't have any brothers or sisters. It gets lonely sometimes."

"One thing's for sure," Benny said in his soft voice. "James never wanted a brother like me. He got teased by his friends because of me. That's why he liked his dog so much. His dog could do things better than me. His dog could count and catch a ball in its mouth. It could fetch things and do all sorts of tricks. That dog was special," Benny said boastfully. "That dog was a lot smarter than me. That dog sort of made up to James for having a brother like me."

"Could the dog talk?" Marcella eyed Figment, who was now stretched out in a long line on the cement floor, head extended onto his front paws, eyes seesawing between her and Benny.

"James said he could," Benny said wide-eyed. "James said if anything ever happened to his dog, he would die."

Marcella knew what James meant. She felt the same way about Figment. About Benny and Judge Willa Scott. About Libby Grimes. She didn't want to lose any of them!

"I suppose that dog is gone now," Marcella said thoughtfully. "Since that was a long time ago."

"Yep." Benny ambled over to the stool he sat on when he did work at his workbench. "The dog got lost. All 'cause of me. James told me never to leave the back gate open. But I was so stupid I must have forgot. Stupid me. Stupid me. James was real mad at me. He was so mad he told me he was going to have the police watch me the rest of my life. Then when I did another stupid thing, they would be right there to get me. Once and for all."

"And nobody ever found the dog?"

"No. Nobody found the dog. He was lost for good. James begged Daddy to put one of them ads in the newspaper so everybody would know his dog was lost. But Daddy wouldn't do it. He said it was wasting good money. We didn't have much money for newspaper ads. So James just walked all over town looking for his dog. He did that every day for a month. After that, he was real mad at Daddy. I guess for not putting that ad in the paper. He was so mad at Daddy he wouldn't talk to him for the longest time. He was mad at me, too. It was like James had died but was still walking around."

Marcella was sure that was the way she would feel, too, if anything ever happened to one of *her* friends. In fact, she was a little worried about leaving Figment with Benny. Still, she had no choice.

"I have a favor to ask you, Benny. My parents don't know about Figment. They don't know I have him. I'm trying to talk them into letting me keep him, but I need a place for him to stay until I do that. Could you keep him here for a while?"

"Me?"

"Sure, Benny. You could look after him. You got him out of my dollhouse, didn't you?"

"Yeah. But that didn't take so long. Suppose he runs away? It would be all my fault! Just like James's dog. And the police would come."

"No, Benny. The police won't come. James only told you that because he was mad at you. I won't call the police. Even if Figment runs away."

Benny made a low, whimpering noise. "I don't know. I don't know. I don't know!"

Marcella thought of something. "The only thing we have to worry about, Benny, is something to feed Figment. I didn't bring any food."

"I get food," Benny said in a higher-pitched voice. "Three times a day. People deliver it to me from a restaurant. James makes them do it. They started doing it after my Daddy died."

"I know, Benny, you told me that. But how

much food do you get? Is there enough for Figment? He eats a lot!"

"I get lots of food. James makes sure."

"Will you do it then? Will you keep Figment?"

Benny didn't say anything for a minute. "You been a good friend, Marcella. Not like those kids that throw rocks at me. I could tell James I take care of a dog. Then maybe he wouldn't come take me away."

Marcella patted Benny on the shoulder. And then she watched him carve another Statue of Liberty.

15

"Marcella, Marcella, wake up!" Mrs. Starbuckle shook Marcella's shoulder until Marcella opened her eyes. It was Sunday morning, so Marcella knew her mother was not waking her up to go to school. "You were having a bad dream," her mother said. "You were shouting something about a dog in a dollhouse."

Marcella sat up in bed. Figment was nowhere in sight. She remembered now. She had taken Figment to Benny's. And she remembered the bad dream.

In her dream, the police had come to get Figment from her. Judge Willa Scott was with them. And Libby Grimes, too. She had no choice but to take them to Benny's, otherwise they were going to feed her to a Venus's-flytrap. But when they got to Benny's, Figment wasn't there. Instead, Benny had carved a huge Statue of Liberty that talked. No one seemed to think it was odd that the Statue of Liberty talked, except Marcella. The Statue of Liberty kept saying, "The dog is in the dollhouse! The dog is in the dollhouse!"

Marcella rubbed her face and blinked. Then, because the dream seemed so real, she hopped out of bed and ran across the room to peer inside the dollhouse. Of course, Figment was not there.

"What's the matter, Marcella?" her mother asked. "You're acting awfully strange."

"Just a bad dream, I guess. Only . . . only I think it was more than just a dream. I think my conscience is trying to talk to me, to tell me something."

"I know what you mean, Marcella. My conscience has been talking to me lately. It's been telling me I haven't been fair. Just because I don't like dogs doesn't mean *you* shouldn't like them. And, well, if you think you still want a dog . . ."

"Do you really mean it?" Marcella dashed across the room and threw her arms around her mother's waist. "I'm so happy! I'll go get Figment!"

"Hey, what's going on in here?" Mr. Starbuckle staggered into Marcella's room, rubbing at his eyes.

"Figment," Mrs. Starbuckle said, looking puzzled. "Why do you have to go get Figment?"

"Let's not have company today, Marcella," Mr. Starbuckle protested. "I had this great idea to go for a picnic in the park. Let's make this a family-only day."

"But Figment is family," Marcella said. "Mom just said I could have a dog if I wanted one. Figment is the dog I want. He's going to be part of our family."

"Figment's a dog?" Mrs. Starbuckle sank onto Marcella's bed, and that's when Marcella said, "Uh-oh" to herself. Marcella had the feeling she had just made a big boo-boo.

"Now wait a minute, young lady," Mr. Starbuckle said. "You told us Figment was a friend of yours from school. A classmate. You don't expect us to believe that a dog came over to play with you the other night, do you? Why, I even talked to Figment on the telephone. What's going on here, Marcella?"

Marcella sank down next to her mother on the bed. No matter what she told her parents about Figment, they were going to think she had tricked them. And she had. Libby Grimes had predicted it: "One of these days, Marcella, your stories are going to get you in big trouble." Now Marcella knew what Libby meant. If ever there was a time she needed her parents to believe her, this was it. But how could they? How could they?

"Figment is a dog I found when I came home from school one day. He asked me for food, so I gave him some. And then he asked to come in the house and I let him. And he stayed up in my room for five days. Only now he's staying with a friend of mine. Because I was afraid you'd find him and be mad and never let him stay again if you found out about him."

"Okay," Mr. Starbuckle said. "So you say you found a stray dog. I get that part. And you hid him in the house here for a few days. That might explain all the missing food. But this part about Figment talking. Marcella, a dog talking?"

"Now wait a minute," Mrs. Starbuckle said. "Who talked to us on the phone the other night?"

"That was me," Marcella admitted. "I pretended to be Figment."

"Okay, so now we're getting somewhere," Mr. Starbuckle said. Then suddenly Marcella's father looked even more puzzled. "You pretended to be a dog talking?"

Marcella nodded her head.

"Now that's just great," Mr. Starbuckle moaned.

"Honey," he said to Marcella's mother, "maybe we need to make that appointment with Doctor Teller after all."

Mrs. Starbuckle heaved a deep sigh. "Marcella, where is this dog now?"

"At Benny's. Benny Slocum's. He lives about four blocks from here."

"Benny Slocum, the retarded man!" Mrs. Starbuckle gasped.

"Don't call him that! He's smart when it comes to carving the Statue of Liberty."

Mrs. Starbuckle's face clouded. "Well, he's not the proper friend for a little girl. I don't want you to go there ever again. You can have a dog if you promise you won't go there."

Marcella glanced down at the floor. Not go see Benny? Ever again? "But Benny is my friend! And what about Figment? He's my friend, too! I'll need to go there to get Figment. I'll have to tell Benny why you won't let me be friends with him. He won't understand. He'll be scared!"

"*I'll* go get Figment," Mr. Starbuckle decided. "If there really is a Figment. And I'll talk to Mr. Slocum."

Marcella felt her face flush. Her parents just didn't believe that Figment was real. They thought she had made him up. And they didn't understand how Benny could be her friend. They didn't understand at all.

"Benny gets scared real easy," Marcella told her father. "He'll think you've come to be mean to him. He'll think you're from the police. Please let *me* go, Daddy. Please?"

"No, Marcella. Your mother is right. You should have friends your own age. And if there is a dog there, he probably belongs to someone else. We'd have to put an ad in the paper and try to find the owner before we could claim him ourselves."

Marcella's hopes sank. But then when she thought about it, she knew her father was right. Judge Scott had told Marcella to place the ad days ago, but Marcella had been too afraid of losing Figment to do it. If Figment belonged to somebody else, it wasn't fair for her to keep him. Now Marcella felt courageous as she described Figment for the ad that her father would drop at the newspaper office while he was out. She was thinking that even if Figment belonged to someone else, at least she would get to keep him a little while longer until that "someone" saw her ad.

While her father was at Benny's to get Figment, Marcella paced the floor. She ran from window to window, hoping to catch a glimpse of her father returning with Figment. And if only Benny would show her dad his Statue of Liberty carvings, Marcella hoped, then maybe Mr. Starbuckle would see Benny differently and let him be friends with her.

"He wouldn't answer the door," Marcella's father announced when he came back minutes later. "I knocked at the garage and he yelled out for me to go away. No dog barked, Marcella."

"But he's there! I know Figment's there with Benny."

"Why don't we just let this thing drop, Marcella? Let's wait a week or two and then see if we can't find a nice puppy."

"That's a good idea, Marcella," Mrs. Starbuckle agreed.

"You don't believe me," Marcella said slowly. "You don't believe Figment is with Benny."

"Considering all the wild stories you've told," Mr. Starbuckle asked, "do you blame us?"

16

"Pssst . . . Marcella!" Libby Grimes whispered in class on Monday. Libby held up a note so Marcella could see it, then she dropped her pencil, retrieved it from the floor, and left the note in its place beside Marcella's desk.

Marcella reluctantly picked up the note. Tammy Collins was watching the whole thing! Was Libby crazy or what?

Marcella unfolded the note and read what Libby had written. "Meet me at Judge Scott's after school," it said. Marcella quickly penciled in underneath Libby's message, "I can't." Then she refolded the note and wrote Libby's name on the outside. She handed the note to Tammy, who sat directly behind her and was supposed to hand it back to Libby, who sat in back of Tammy.

Marcella knew that Tammy would look at the

note before she passed it on to Libby. When she read the note, Tammy would be satisfied that Marcella was not trying to be friends with Libby. Maybe now Tammy wouldn't try to bother Benny.

Anyway, Marcella didn't want to go to Judge Scott's. Even though she was forbidden, she had plans to go to Benny's after school to get Figment.

After school, Marcella noticed that the Terrific Three didn't even try to follow Libby to Judge Scott's. They were still too afraid Judge Scott was a witch. They didn't bother following Marcella either. Ordinarily, Marcella would have felt hurt by being ignored. But today she was glad the Terrific Three didn't want to play with her. She needed to talk to Benny alone. Today, she would take Figment home with her. Would her parents be surprised when they found out there really *was* a Figment!

When Marcella entered Benny's garage, Benny wasn't working on another Statue of Liberty. He was building a house. A house that looked a lot like her dollhouse, only it was bigger and much roomier since it didn't have walls and a staircase.

"It's a doghouse," Benny explained, his eyes lighting up. "For Figment."

Marcella walked all around the house. She had to admire the great job Benny had done building the house. But why had Benny built the house when she'd told him he'd only get to keep Figment for a few days?

"That's nice, Benny," Marcella said, patting Figment's head. "Except I've come to take Figment home with me. My parents said I can keep him. My father came to get Figment yesterday. Why wouldn't you open the door?"

Benny put down his hammer. "Uh-oh, Marcella, I thought your father was the police." But when he said it, he didn't look at Marcella. "You said Figment was staying with me for a while. You take him now, he won't get to try out the house."

Marcella felt terrible. "The fact is, Benny," Marcella stammered, ". . . the fact is, I really don't know who Figment belongs to. He could belong to somebody else. That's why I've put an ad in the newspaper, trying to find out who he belongs to. I only get to keep him if nobody answers the ad."

Marcella's conscience nagged at her. It wasn't completely true that Marcella had placed her own ad in the newspaper because she wanted to find Figment's owner. She never would have done it if

Judge Scott hadn't pointed out it was the right thing to do and if her parents hadn't insisted. They would never let her keep Figment until they were sure he was a stray.

"And I don't get to keep him at all," Benny moaned. "See, I had it all planned. I'd build the house. And James would come and see what I'd done. And then he'd know I really like dogs. And it wasn't me that lost his dog that one time. And he'd see I can take real good care of a dog. Then maybe he'd let me have my own dog. He might even let me stay here to live."

"I never thought you wanted a dog, Benny."

"Oh, yeah. I've wanted a dog. But my daddy never would let me have one. He said I couldn't take care of it proper. And then when he died, well, James said he wanted me to come live with him. They don't let you have dogs where James lives."

Marcella studied Benny's blinking blue eyes. She looked at Figment, who was sitting at Benny's side, his bushy tail sweeping the cement floor with contentment. How could she take Figment away from Benny?

"But Benny, I miss Figment. He's my best friend. He helps me do my homework. And I can talk to him when there's nobody else around to talk to."

"But you got other friends. You got parents, and friends at school. And Judge Scott. I got nobody, Marcella. I got nobody but you and Figment."

Benny was right, Marcella thought with surprise, but Marcella just couldn't give up yet. "But, Benny ... I told my parents about Figment. If I don't bring him home with me, they're going to think I made him up."

"Please," Benny whined. "It's important. I want to show James. James is coming soon to take me away. He has Mrs. Jacobs checking on me every day. He makes sure people deliver food to me three times a day. James says I will be better off with him. He doesn't think I can do anything. James is all wrong about me. I have to show him. I have to show him!"

"Okay, Benny," Marcella said, finally. "Keep Figment. Just until James comes. But if somebody answers my newspaper ad, we'll both have to give Figment up. You understand that, don't you?"

"I understand."

Figment must have understood, too, because he cowered in the front door of the doghouse, turned, and peeked out at them. If Figment talked to Marcella at that moment, she was sure he would say, "It's a nice house, Marcella, but I'd rather go home with you."

Yet when Marcella looked at Benny, he was smiling and he seemed to be hearing something different from Figment.

Marcella shuffled out of the garage, tears forming in her eyes. That's when she ran smack-dab into Libby Grimes. "What are *you* doing here? Spying on me?"

"Okay, yeah, I'm spying on you," Libby admitted. "I have to spy on you. Otherwise, you don't tell me anything. I thought we were friends!"

"Some friend you are," Marcella complained. "You told me you were going to Judge Scott's."

"Well, if I went to Judge Scott's, who would be here to see that dog with Benny and tell you that you have the wrong dog? That dog isn't the missing Riverview dog. See. Look here." Libby pulled out the newspaper clipping. "They don't look the same. Marcella, what's going on? You've got to tell me the truth about everything. Start from the beginning, and don't leave anything out."

Marcella glowered at Libby. "Libby Grimes, not only are you acting like a detective, but you're beginning to talk like a detective, too. I'll tell you the

114

truth about everything, but you've got to promise to cross your heart and die a thousand deaths not to tell."

"Forget the detective. A good friend never breaks a trust."

Marcella smiled.

17

Libby didn't say anything after Marcella told her about Figment. She didn't say anything all the next day at school. Marcella thought she would bust if Libby didn't say something soon, but when her friend finally did say something as they walked together away from Riverview Elementary, Marcella didn't like what Libby had to say.

"I think we should still call this number in the ad," Libby said, studying the newspaper clipping about the missing Riverview dog. By now the clipping was wrinkled and tearing apart because Libby had studied it so much.

"No," Marcella said.

"Why not?"

"Well, because . . . because . . . suppose whoever is looking for that dog doesn't find their dog, but they go ahead and say that Figment belongs to them."

"That's ridiculous, Marcella."

"What's so ridiculous about it?"

"Would you claim a dog that wasn't yours?" Libby swallowed thickly. "Yes, well, I guess you've already claimed a dog that isn't yours."

"See. Then. It's not so ridiculous. But I'll tell you something that *is* ridiculous."

"What?"

"The picture of that dog," Marcella said, snatching the clipping away from Libby. She brought the clipping to her face, till her nose was almost touching it. "I can't put my finger on it, but this picture doesn't look right."

"I know what you mean. It looks old. I mean, it doesn't look like it was taken very recently."

"I know what it is!" Marcella said suddenly. "It's that car in the background. Look at it real careful. Have you ever seen a car like that?"

Libby yanked back the clipping, looked, and shook her head. "Nobody I know of has a car like that. It's the fenders. They're like wings."

"That's because it's an old car," Marcella said, snatching the clipping back. "I think I saw an old car like that once in a movie."

"How old is it?"

"Older than us."

117

"That's not so old . . . for a car."

"Look!" Marcella pointed to a white object in the picture that sat on a front-porch step of a house in the background of the picture. "What's that?"

Libby looked close. "I can't tell. I wish I had a magnifying glass. If I had a magnifying glass, I could tell."

"You have one at home?"

Libby shook her head and asked, "Do you?"

Marcella shrugged. "I don't think so. But I bet I know someone who would have one."

Marcella didn't even have to say Judge Scott's name. Both girls took off running for Judge Scott's house. But when they rounded the corner of the school, they found themselves headed straight into the path of the Terrific Three.

"Uh-oh," Marcella said, slowing. "They've seen us. What should we do?"

"Tell them there's a swarm of bees following us?"

Marcella couldn't believe Libby said that, that Libby would even suggest they lie to the Terrific Three. "Let's don't tell them anything. Then we don't have to lie."

So that's what they did. They ran straight past

Tammy Collins and Jill Kramer and Linda Cappanelli. They ran so fast, the Terrific Three didn't have a chance to ask them anything. The Terrific Three just stood there dumbfounded, looking in the direction Marcella and Libby had run from, trying to figure out what was wrong.

Marcella and Libby knocked on the door of Judge Scott's greenhouse, huffing and puffing out of breath. Judge Scott hobbled to the door, peeked out at them through the glass, and scolded, "Think you can bother a dying woman any time you feel like it!"

"We need your help, Judge Scott," Marcella said breathlessly.

Judge Scott opened the door. "Hummph. Where were you when I needed *your* help? My plants still need repotting. I'm going to die in five days, don't you know!"

"But when we were doing that the other day — "

Marcella elbowed Libby in the side. "That's why we're here, Judge Scott. Show us what you want us to do."

Judge Scott sniffed, her nose wiggling like that of a discerning rat. "Same thing as before," she said, tapping her cane along a row of terra-cotta pots.

Then she waved it over the entire two tables of plants. "All of these have to be done before I die."

Marcella looked at Libby. Libby looked at Marcella. How would they ever accomplish such a task in five days?

"Do you have a magnifying glass, Judge Scott?" Libby asked.

"You don't need a magnifying glass to repot plants."

"No, but we need it to look at this picture," Marcella said, pulling out the newspaper clipping and showing it to Judge Scott again. "See, Libby and I have this theory that this picture was taken a long time ago. On account of the old car in the background. And if we could only tell what this white thing is on this porch across the street — "

"It's a bottle of milk," Judge Scott said.

Marcella and Libby exchanged glances.

"Thirty years ago, there used to be a milk-delivery service in Riverview," Judge Scott said. "People didn't buy milk in cartons at the grocery store. It was delivered in glass bottles right to their doors."

Marcella and Libby exchanged another glance. "Then that picture was taken thirty years ago?" Marcella asked.

"And that dog was missing thirty years ago?" Libby asked.

"Why would anybody still be looking for that dog now?" Marcella asked.

"Who would run an ad in the paper with a picture of a dog that was missing thirty years ago?" Libby asked. "And offer a thousand-dollar reward for a dog that couldn't possibly still be alive?"

"Good questions," Judge Scott said. "You're finally beginning to use your brains. To say nothing of the use of obvious evidence." But then Judge Scott sank slowly into her rocking chair with a noise that sounded a lot like the air escaping from a balloon. "I'll answer those questions. Somebody," she said slowly, "who's going to die in five days."

"You?" the girls asked together.

Judge Scott nodded. "It was the only way I could think of to find the little boy who used to own that dog. It wasn't the dog I was looking for, really, but the boy who once owned him. Even though he would be all grown up now, he would recognize the photo he took of the dog he owned so long ago. If I had advertised a 'found' dog, every owner looking for a lost dog that fit that dog's description would be calling me. I didn't want that."

"But I don't understand, Judge Scott," Libby

said, still intent on getting at the truth. "Why do you have to find the boy . . . I mean, the man who used to own that dog?"

Judge Scott sniffed. "So I won't have to die with a guilty conscience."

"What did you do to him?" Libby asked.

"I lied to him," Judge Scott said in a low voice, so low and so different from her usual voice that Marcella wasn't even sure the words came from the judge.

"But he wouldn't be a little boy anymore," Libby said. "He'd be all grown up after thirty years."

"You think that makes any difference!" Judge Scott roared. "You think he doesn't remember that he lost his dog! Even after all these years? Children don't forget things like that. Even when they're grown up! You think I don't remember that his father brought the dog to me to sell the animal when he hadn't even told the boy that that was what he was going to do! You think I don't remember buying the dog so the man's other son could go to a special school!"

"But you couldn't have known the dog belonged to the little boy," Marcella reasoned gently. "The man didn't tell you, did he?"

"It wasn't your fault," Libby argued.

"It was my fault that I didn't ask the man more about the dog," Judge Scott said slowly. "It was my fault when the little boy came looking for the dog that I didn't tell him I had bought the dog and given it to my nephew who lived in Washington at the time." Judge Scott was silent for a moment. "I will never forget that little boy's face. The way he looked when I said I didn't have the dog. The way his little hand reached out to me with the picture of the dog. He had spent his last dime having copies of the picture made so he could give them out to people. By then, I knew what had happened. But I didn't tell him. My silence was as much of a lie as if I'd told the boy I'd never seen the dog before!"

Marcella stopped potting the plant in front of her. "Judge Scott," she began carefully. "I know who the little boy is . . . was . . . that you're looking for."

"She does not," Libby said, eyeing Marcella, thinking it was another one of her stories.

"Yes, I do. I know who he is! He's Benny's brother, James!"

"Prove it, Marcella." Libby said it as if she were sure that Marcella was making it all up to seem important.

Could Libby be jealous? Marcella wondered. Because Marcella knew something Libby didn't? Marcella, the Detective. It had a nice ring to it. But maybe not to Libby.

Marcella told them what Benny had said about James having a dog long ago and how the dog was lost. She told about her visit with Doctor Bingham and how surprised he was that she knew the name of the boy who was his playmate long ago. A boy named James, who owned a talking dog. "And you know what?" Marcella asked, when she was through with her story. "Benny thinks that he was the one who lost James's dog. But it was his father who brought the dog here to Judge Scott. Benny didn't lose the dog, after all."

"Another lie perpetuated by a truthless deed!" Judge Scott said, snorting. "I must have his phone number. This James. I must set the wrong right before I die."

"I can get it for you," Marcella offered.

"After we've repotted all the plants," Libby said, sighing deeply at the sight of so many pots yet to go.

"Then go get it!" Judge Scott shrieked, waving at them. "Off with you. Shoo. Shoo. Thirty years is as long as a dying woman can wait."

"But what about the plants? What about the Venus's-flytrap you promised we could feed?"

Libby asked. "I was going to ask you if we could take it to school for our report."

"I'll take it under advisement," Judge Scott said.

"What's advisement?" Libby asked.

Marcella grabbed Libby's arm and yanked her out of the greenhouse. Sometimes even detectives can ask too many questions.

18

It was too late to go to Benny's when Marcella and Libby left Judge Willa Scott's. So they decided to go there first thing after school the next day.

Marcella's stomach did flip-flops for joy in anticipation of seeing Figment again. But then, at home, the telephone would ring, and Marcella would feel a tapeworm eating at the insides of her stomach till she found out who it was, fearing it was someone calling about her ad, wanting Figment back. Then when it was someone calling for one of her parents, the tapeworm would disappear.

A couple of times, Libby called to ask if anyone had answered the ad. Marcella knew it was Libby even though Libby started out by saying, "This is Figment, your dog, speaking. Can I come home now?" Marcella knew Libby wasn't making fun of her by pretending to be a talking dog. She was just trying to act crazy because they were both so nervous about how things were going to turn out.

At school the next day, Marcella and Libby worked together on their science report. When they were finished, Mrs. Crandall asked them if they had learned anything about the Venus's-flytrap that they hadn't known before. She asked them to share it with the rest of the class.

"The Venus's-flytrap is a very misunderstood plant," Marcella began. "Some people think that the plant can bite and chew. But that is not true. The Venus's-flytrap does not chew anything. When it feels an insect on its leaves, little hairs cause the leaves to quickly bend in half and trap the insect. And the Venus's-flytrap does not digest the insect because it needs meat. It digests the insect in order to get a salt called nitrate that it needs to live. It's funny how people are scared of the Venus's-flytrap until they learn the truth."

"Very good, Marcella," Mrs. Crandall said, when Marcella was finished. "You have done an excellent report."

Marcella beamed. Then Libby reported that she was going to bring a Venus's-flytrap to school soon to show the class how the plant traps insects. Everybody gasped with pleasure. All except the Terrific Three. They glowered at Libby and Marcella.

"They're just jealous because we had the best science report," Libby whispered to Marcella.

Maybe so, Marcella thought, but she had a jittery feeling that the Terrific Three were thinking about ways to get back at Marcella and Libby for having a good report together. And what about Tammy's threat to bother Benny if Marcella continued to be friends with Libby?

Marcella didn't think about the Terrific Three again until Mrs. Crandall asked Marcella and Libby to stay after school. Marcella didn't want to stay after school. She and Libby had planned to go to Benny's. To get James's phone number for Judge Willa Scott. Also, she wanted to see Figment!

"I wonder," Mrs. Crandall started out. "I wonder if you should have promised the class to bring a Venus's-flytrap to school after all."

"Why do you wonder that?" Libby asked.

"Because the Venus's-flytrap is a very hard plant to find. The class would be very disappointed if you couldn't bring one. In fact, a few class members don't believe you can."

Marcella looked at Libby, and Libby looked at

Marcella. They knew who Mrs. Crandall meant by "a few class members."

"Don't worry, Mrs. Crandall," Libby told their teacher. "The person who has the Venus's-flytrap is thinking about whether to let us borrow it. We'll know today or tomorrow whether we can bring it."

"We can bring it if she doesn't die first," Marcella added.

Mrs. Crandall's green eyes widened. "Perhaps we'd better forget about the Venus's-flytrap. Some of the class say they might not come to school with a Venus's-flytrap in the room."

"Oh, no, Mrs. Crandall," Libby begged. "Please let us bring it. Like our report says, it's really not a dangerous plant."

"Those members of the class who told you that are the dangerous ones," Marcella said. "They're telling stories to get their way."

"Funny you should mention that, Marcella," Mrs. Crandall said. "I've noticed a strange thing happening in this class. You aren't telling stories anymore. And children who didn't used to tell stories are. Why do you suppose that is?"

Marcella thought for a moment. She tried to answer Mrs. Crandall's question with as much wisdom as Judge Willa Scott. "I think they are doing it for the same reasons I used to do it. Because they feel left out."

Mrs. Crandall smiled. "I think you are right, Marcella."

After that, Mrs. Crandall let Marcella and Libby leave. They ran as fast as they could to Benny's. But when they got there, Benny was standing in the doorway of his garage, holding his head and moaning. "He's gone. He's gone. Figment's gone!"

"What happened, Benny?" Marcella gasped. "Where is Figment?"

"It's all my fault," Benny moaned. "I thought it was you knocking on the door, so I opened it. Why would anyone say it was you when it wasn't?"

"Who was it, Benny?" Libby asked.

"It was ... it was ... I don't know, I don't know!"

"Was it three girls about our age, Benny?" Marcella asked.

"Yes. Three girls. Three mean, mean girls. They threw rocks at me. They called me names. They called me Retard. Why did they do that? Why did they have to call me names and throw rocks at me?" Benny shook his head in disbelief.

"Because they were mad at us, Benny," Marcella explained. "They were mad at us for having a good science report. They're mad at me for being friends with Libby."

"But I haven't done anything to them!"

"It's all my fault, Benny," Marcella told him. "I should have stayed away from you so they wouldn't do this to you. And I should never have brought Figment here. I knew this might happen. I knew those girls might be mean to you."

"But what about Figment?" Benny moaned. "He wasn't afraid of them. He ran after them. Even when they threw rocks. Now he's gone. I lost him! I lost him!"

"We'll find him, Benny," Libby assured him. "Figment's probably still chasing those meanies. I hope he bites them!"

"No. No. No, no, no." Benny ambled back inside the garage. "The police might come if Figment bites them. They're gonna say I made Figment bite them. Please go away," he begged, shutting the door. "Go away, go away!"

"We'll be back, Benny," Marcella called through the door. "We'll find Figment."

But when Marcella looked at Libby, and when

they both looked up and down the deserted alley, she wasn't sure she could keep her promise. She was suddenly terribly sorry she had made such a promise to Benny. Promises meant something to Benny. For the first time in her life, promises meant something to Marcella.

"Wait! Marcella!" Libby called to Marcella, who without saying a word had dashed down the alley, hoping to catch a glimpse of Figment. "We have to plan what to do!"

Marcella didn't want to plan how to find Figment. She wanted to find him. Quick! But she stopped and turned to Libby. "We're wasting time. You look that way, and I'll go this way." She pointed out opposite directions.

"I have another idea," Libby said. "Let's go find the Terrific Three. They might know where Figment is."

Marcella didn't want to go find the Terrific Three. The last thing she wanted to do was talk to them. Those brats! Those spoiled babies! Those bullies! Somebody should talk to their parents instead of them. That would fix them! She told Libby how she felt about the Terrific Three. "Telling

133

their parents on them would be too good for them. We should throw rocks at them and call *them* names. See how *they* like it!"

"You aren't being a very good detective, Marcella. A good detective keeps a cool head. We want to find Figment, right? Well, the best way to do that is to find the Terrific Three and question them."

"I'll question them," Marcella said, her voice still edged with anger. "I'll ask them who they think they are acting the way they did to Benny. I'll tell them I'm going to call the police and report them!"

"That won't make them stop calling Benny names or throwing rocks if they feel like it. And it won't make them tell us what happened to Figment. We have to try being friendly first."

Marcella rolled her eyes at Libby. Sometimes Libby Grimes made her almost as mad as the Terrific Three did. But Marcella followed Libby to Tammy Collins's house. Three bicycles were parked out front. And Marcella thought she saw the curtain at the front window move when she and Libby knocked on the door.

Mrs. Collins answered the door. Marcella liked Mrs. Collins because she was a stay-at-home mother who was always bringing party treats to school on holidays, and she always said hello to all of Tammy's classmates.

"Why, hello, Libby . . . Marcella. Tammy has friends over right now, but you're welcome to come in anyway." Mrs. Collins smiled broadly, and Marcella wished Tammy were as soft-spoken and genuinely pleasant as her mother. She wondered if Mrs. Collins knew how mean Tammy could be when something didn't go her way.

"We're looking for a dog, Mrs. Collins," Libby explained in as sweet a voice as Tammy's mother's. "We're sure Tammy and Jill and Linda might know something about the dog because they were the last ones who saw him."

"Why don't you step in?" Mrs. Collins asked. "Maybe the girls can help you."

While Marcella and Libby shifted from one leg to the other, Mrs. Collins disappeared to the back of the house and returned with the Terrific Three. Marcella wondered if Mrs. Collins noticed that the Terrific Three shuffled reluctantly in front of her like glue that refused to come out of a bottle. They wouldn't look Marcella or Libby in the eye, either.

"We need help finding Figment," Libby said.

"He's the dog that chased you from Benny Slocum's. He belongs to Marcella. He's not the missing Riverview dog."

"How do we know you're not lying?" Tammy asked.

"Why, Tammy," Mrs. Collins gasped, looking puzzled, "Marcella and Libby wouldn't lie about something like that. Whatever made you say that?"

Tammy shrugged. "We don't know where he is."

"But you can help them look," Mrs. Collins said, sounding surprised.

"We don't want to help them look," Tammy said flatly.

Libby pulled out the clipping of the missing Riverview dog. "See. This dog and Figment are not the same. But it's real important that we find Figment. Remember my birthday party I'm having in six days? Well, see, I'm having this contest at the party." Then Libby stopped, which was unfortunate because everybody in the room was looking right at her when she mentioned her birthday party and the contest. Libby stopped because it seemed like she couldn't think of the rest of what to tell. "You tell them, Marcella."

Marcella felt like she'd been suddenly dipped in

boiling water and then plunged into a frozen lake. What was the matter with Libby anyway? Why was she suddenly talking about a contest at her birthday party? Why was she leaving it to Marcella to explain about the contest that Marcella knew nothing about? Was it a surprise birthday contest? In that case, Marcella explained, "Uh, see, it's not a best-costume contest for people. It's going to be a best-costume contest for our pets."

"Yeah," Libby agreed, nodding her head and smiling. "That's what it's going to be. Only I can't have that kind of party unless everyone can bring a pet dressed in a costume. It wouldn't be fair. Now that Marcella has lost Figment, I may have to call the whole thing off."

"Oh, don't do that," Jill Kramer piped up. "I've never been to a birthday party like that before. It sounds like fun!"

Linda Cappanelli's eyes lit up. "I have the perfect costume for my cat, Mississippi. You won't guess it in a million years!"

"Shh, then, don't tell," Libby said. "It's supposed to be a surprise."

"It sounds silly," Tammy Collins snorted. "A birthday-party costume contest with our pets?"

"You don't have a pet either?" Marcella asked.

"Of course, I do," Tammy sniffed. "I have the best pet of all. I have a cocker spaniel, Buttons."

"I know what costume would be perfect for Buttons!" Jill Kramer said.

"Too bad a good idea has to go to waste." Libby shrugged. "If we don't find Figment, there won't be any contest. There might not even be a party. I couldn't have the party with Marcella's dog lost."

"He followed us here. Marcella's dog," Jill explained. "We ran into the house, and then he just walked away that way," she said, pointing in the direction Figment had gone.

"Maybe if you all go looking, you can find him," Mrs. Collins suggested. "Hurry. You might still catch sight of him."

Five bodies scrambled to the door and then streamed out of it, spreading out in all directions. Libby, who was good at directing people, divided them up, each with her own street to look for Figment. They looked until suppertime. No Figment.

They met back at Tammy's house. "We'll help you look again tomorrow after school," Tammy offered. The other girls nodded.

The next three days after school, the Terrific Three helped Marcella and Libby look for Figment. Since the three girls were helping them look, not once did Marcella or Libby say that Figment's being lost was the fault of the Terrific Three in the first place. Not once did any of the Terrific Three accuse Marcella of lying or try to tell Libby she was wrong for being friends with Marcella. The five of them spent recesses at school huddled together, trying to think of different places to look for Figment.

On the third day, Marcella was so worried about not finding Figment that she went to Judge Scott's house to tell her that Figment was missing. Since Judge Scott had lots of experience with missing dogs, Marcella hoped she would have something wise to say about what to do. After Marcella explained that she'd forgotten to get James's phone number in all the excitement, Judge Scott had questions for Marcella.

"Did you place the 'dog found' ad in the paper like I told you? It might help find the dog now."

Marcella nodded.

"Have you looked all over town? Talked to people who might have seen Figment?"

Marcella nodded.

"Well, then. Do you feel you've done everything you could possibly do?"

"Yes," Marcella said truthfully.

That seemed to please Judge Scott more than all the things Marcella had done to find Figment. She smiled and rocked contentedly in her rocker.

When Marcella came home from Judge Scott's, Benny's doghouse was sitting in her backyard. Marcella hoped that meant Benny wasn't upset about losing Figment anymore. And she wanted to hope that the doghouse was a sign that when she found Figment, she could keep him. After all, no one had answered her ad to claim Figment. Not one single call! Now, if only she could find him!

But the doghouse probably definitely meant that Benny was moving away with James. Because of that, Marcella missed Figment more than ever. It wasn't fair to lose them both. It wasn't fair! It wasn't fair!

20

Marcella peered through the wood-slatted fence of Benny's backyard. A large orange moving van had been parked close to the back door of Benny's tiny house. Benny and a strange man were carrying things out of the house and loading them into the van.

The strange man looked a lot like Benny, only he was slimmer, and he didn't blink his eyes as much. Marcella knew he must be Benny's brother, James.

She wanted to say good-bye to Benny, but she wondered if that was a good idea. Maybe it was better for Benny if she didn't say good-bye. Maybe she would only remind him that Figment had been lost. Maybe she would remind him that he was leaving his home and Marcella, his friend. And James might be angry if Marcella caused Benny to hold his head and moan.

But she wouldn't have to mention Figment at all, Marcella reasoned, although she was supposed to be looking for him at that very moment, the same as the Terrific Three and Libby Grimes. She had thought it was a good idea to come back to Benny's to see if Figment had turned up there. But now, seeing Benny . . .

"Marcella! Marcella!" Libby Grimes yelled, racing up to her and gasping for air. "We have to get help! There's something wrong with Judge Scott!"

Libby yelled so loud that Benny and James turned away from their task of loading a stuffed chair into the van to look at the two girls.

"Help!" Marcella called to them. "Help! Help! Help!"

Benny and James dropped the chair and came running over to Marcella and Libby. "What's the matter?" James asked.

"It's Judge Willa Scott," Libby said, still puffing out of breath. "I went there to ask her for the Venus's-flytrap plant. There's something wrong with her. She just sits in her rocker. She looks real sick."

"Show us," James said.

The four of them ran to Judge Willa Scott's

greenhouse. They found Judge Scott where Libby had left her, sitting in her rocker. Her gnarled hand lay on her cane, but she wasn't tapping it as usual. She was staring off into space. She was mumbling something that none of them could understand.

James bent down on one knee close to Judge Scott's rocker. "Judge Scott," he said softly, tenderly. "Do you remember me? I'm James Slocum. I lived in Riverview a long time ago. Can you tell me what's wrong?"

Finally, slowly and so softly they could barely hear her, Judge Scott said, "There's nothing wrong now. I've been waiting for you to come, James Slocum. I've been waiting to tell you the truth. I can't die until I tell you about your dog."

"It's okay, Judge Scott. Don't talk anymore. I'm going to go call an ambulance." James straightened up and then disappeared into Judge Scott's house.

"Is she really going to die?" Benny asked, his eyes blinking faster now.

"Not until I'm ready," Judge Scott mumbled.

"What does she mean by that?" Benny asked, wide-eyed.

"Questions," Judge Scott mumbled. "Always so many questions."

"I don't want anybody to die," Benny said, holding his head.

"Marcella . . . Libby," Judge Scott said weakly. "Find the boxes under the tables. Benny can help you load them with plants."

Marcella and Libby didn't question why they should begin putting Judge Scott's plants into boxes. They understood that it gave Benny something to do besides think about Judge Scott dying.

James returned from making the phone call. He stooped down next to Judge Scott's chair again. "Hang on, Judge Scott. The ambulance is on its way."

"You've been more help to me than I ever was to you, James," Judge Scott whispered, her left hand shakily moving from the arm of her chair to rest upon James's hand. "That dog you were looking for so long ago . . . do you remember him?"

James smiled. "I remember him. I'll never forget him."

"Your father sold him to me. But don't blame your father. He was only doing it for your brother."

"I know. He told me about it when he died. I don't blame Benny anymore. I stopped blaming Benny a long time ago. I hope Benny will see that. He's going to come live with me. I don't blame my father either. I can understand now why he did it."

"But you remember that dog," Judge Scott said. "You'll never forget that dog."

"No, I'll never forget that dog."

"He had a good home, James. I gave the dog to my nephew. The dog was well taken care of. He had a good life."

"It helps me to hear that."

"I need to hear you say you forgive me for lying to you. I need that before I die."

The back door of the greenhouse flew open, and two men in white uniforms carrying a stretcher scurried to Judge Scott. They lifted her out of her rocking chair onto the stretcher. But her hand wouldn't let go of James.

"I forgive you," James said. But still the hand wouldn't let go.

"Enough to see that the children at the school get my plants?"

"Enough to do that," James said softly.

Judge Scott's hand released James, but she grabbed the hem of Marcella's dress as she passed. She looked Marcella directly in the eye and smiled. "This time the dog is coming home. And that's the truth!"

Then her hand released Marcella, and the paramedics whisked her out the door and into the ambulance. Marcella ran after her, wanting to ask questions. How did Judge Scott know Figment was coming home? Did she know where he was? What made her say such a thing? Why did Judge Scott have to die right now? Couldn't she wait until Figment was back? Till Marcella could tell Judge Scott that Figment had talked to her? What would Judge Scott say about that?

The four of them stood there limply as the ambulance sped away. Finally, James turned back to the greenhouse and said, "Let's get the plants into boxes and I'll bring the van down to load them up."

"Is she going to die, James?" Benny asked. "Is Judge Scott really going to die?"

Marcella and Libby watched James to see how he was going to answer Benny, even though they knew the truth about Judge Willa Scott themselves and didn't really have to hear somebody say what they already knew.

"Yes, Benny," James said. "But Judge Scott is lucky. She got to tell everyone good-bye."

"I'm lucky, too," Benny said, reaching into his pocket and pulling out one of his Statue of Liberty carvings. He handed it to Marcella. Marcella wiped a tear from her cheek and held tightly to the Statue of Liberty.

Then the four of them went back inside the greenhouse and carefully put all of Judge Scott's plants into boxes.

Mrs. Crandall couldn't believe all the plants that James and Benny brought to school before they left for Washington, D.C. "What a wonderful gift," she said. "But whatever are we going to do with them all?"

"Maybe we should adopt some of them out," Marcella suggested. "You know. Everyone in fourth grade can have their own plant to take home." But remembering Judge Scott, she said, "Except anyone adopting a plant must know how to take care of it."

"That's a wonderful idea, Marcella," Mrs. Crandall said. Then during science class, she called for volunteers to look up and identify each of the fifty plants and make up instructions on how to take care of them. Everyone in the class was assigned two plants.

At the end of the day, Mrs. Crandall said that

anyone wishing to adopt a plant could take one home. Everyone in the class raised their hands to adopt plants. Tammy Collins's hand stayed up longer than the rest.

"Mrs. Crandall," Tammy said. "I think Marcella should get to choose her plant first. She's lost her dog. She needs the most special plant in order to go to Libby's birthday-party pet contest tomorrow." Everybody looked at Tammy funny, because they couldn't believe Tammy had suggested Marcella be first to choose.

Marcella couldn't believe Tammy expected her to dress up one of Judge Scott's plants for Libby's birthday party!

Marcella didn't really want a plant. She wanted Figment. But she knew that Libby wanted Rasputin, the Venus's-flytrap, and if she didn't choose Rasputin, it was a sure thing whoever got to choose second would.

Marcella went to the metal shelf that spanned the length of the room where the plants had been arranged. She picked up Rasputin, walked over to Libby's desk, and placed the Venus's-flytrap in front of Libby.

Libby beamed at Marcella.

Nobody in the room said it was unfair for Marcella to give her choice to Libby. And when it was Libby's turn to choose a plant, she chose Herbert, the geranium, and gave it to Marcella. None of the Terrific Three said anything. That was because they weren't the Terrific Three anymore. They and Libby and Marcella were now the Fabulous Five, Marcella's favorite number. The name was Marcella's idea.

After school, the Fabulous Five huddled together outside, only Marcella didn't huddle much, because she didn't feel much like huddling.

"Maybe I'd better just have a regular birthday party," Libby suggested when it was obvious to everyone Marcella would be left out of the fun of the pet-costume party idea.

"I know!" Jill Kramer suggested. "Let's get Marcella a puppy. My neighbor's dog has puppies. Marcella could choose one of those."

Marcella shook her head. "I already told my parents I didn't want a puppy. I can't go back on my word."

"They'd understand," Linda Cappanelli said.

"You ought to see those puppies, Marcella," Jill said with wide eyes. "They're cocker spaniels. Almost as cute as Tammy's dog, Buttons."

"We could go by there and just look," Libby

said, trying to coax Marcella. "It never hurts to look."

Marcella shook her head emphatically. They didn't understand. She didn't want a cocker spaniel! She didn't want a puppy! She wanted Figment!

"No, no, no. A thousand times no," she said, and she took off running.

Marcella ran to Benny's workshop-garage before she remembered that Benny no longer lived there. She ran to Judge Scott's greenhouse. She knew that Judge Scott had really died and was no longer there at the greenhouse, but she found comfort being where Judge Scott had been when she'd said that Figment was going to come home. She sat outside of Judge Scott's greenhouse until she could tell by the position of the sun that her parents would be home by now. She just couldn't go home until they were there.

"Marcella! Where have you been?" her mother greeted her. "We've been waiting and waiting for you to get home."

By "we" her mother meant herself and a strange woman, who sat on the sofa in the Starbuckle living room.

"Marcella, this is Amelia Grandy. She found a stray dog the other day, and then she saw your ad in the paper, which sounded like the dog she found."

"Figment? You found Figment?"

"Well, we don't know if it's Figment," Mrs. Starbuckle said. "I couldn't say for sure, because I've never seen Figment. That's why we were waiting for you."

"Where is he?"

Mrs. Grandy stood up. "He's out in the car with my son, Daniel. I tried to talk Daniel into staying home when I brought the dog over for you to look at." Mrs. Grandy glanced down at the floor. "Daniel's going to be crushed if the dog is the one in your ad. He's become really attached to it." She tittered nervously. "He says the dog talks to him." Her eyes rolled around the room, avoiding Marcella and her mother. "Daniel's been awfully sick this past year. He doesn't get to go to school like other children, so this dog has become important to him. He treats the dog like another person. I tried to keep them separated . . . so Daniel wouldn't get attached . . . until we knew for sure . . ." She shrugged. "I tried, but they're like a magnet and metal. Always together."

The way Mrs. Grandy talked about her son, Marcella hoped the dog in the back of the blue station wagon out front wasn't Figment. But when the three of them walked out to the car, Marcella spotted Figment's familiar head snuggled into the arm of Daniel Grandy, who looked pale and thin and afraid of Marcella.

Marcella walked up to Daniel's side of the car and looked through the window at the two of them. Figment lifted his head and reached his long nose out to her. He licked her hand where it rested on the window frame of the car.

"Are you going to take him away from me?" Daniel asked Marcella.

"What's his name?"

"Cracker. I call him that because he really likes crackers."

"I know." Marcella reached in to stroke Figment's head.

"And he talks."

"What's he talk about?"

"Oh, mainly about baseball. Cracker knows all the big-league hitters. His favorite players are the same as my favorite players. We collect baseball cards together."

Marcella nodded and then brushed at her eyes with the back of her arm.

"Are you going to take him away from me?"

Daniel asked again, looking directly at Marcella with his big brown eyes.

Mrs. Grandy looked as anxious to hear Marcella's answer as Daniel.

"He looks happy. Like he belongs with you." Marcella's voice wavered, as she struggled to find the courage she knew was somewhere deep down inside of her. "Maybe you could keep him. At least until we see if anybody claims him."

"And if nobody claims him?" Daniel asked.

Marcella swallowed a thick lump. "If nobody claims him . . . If nobody claims him, he's yours."

Mrs. Grandy wilted with relief. She skittered to the driver's side of the car, waved a thankful goodbye, and disappeared inside the car.

Marcella watched the car pull away. To help her be brave, her fingers traced Benny's Statue of Liberty in her jacket pocket. When the car was gone, Marcella took the statue out of her pocket and looked at it.

"What is it, Marcella?" her mother asked, watching Marcella turn the carving over and over in her hand.

"Something Benny gave me," she said, handing the carving to her mother. "I pretend it's a good-luck charm. I guess it worked. It brought Figment home to me."

Mrs. Starbuckle's face fell. She wrapped her arm around Marcella's shoulders and squeezed her tight.

"Judge Willa Scott told me Figment would come home," Marcella said, "but she never told me I'd give Figment up. It might have been easier if she'd told me."

Mrs. Starbuckle held Marcella close and stroked the top of her head. "Maybe that's something you had to find out yourself, Marcella."

Marcella nodded. Side by side, she and her mother walked back inside the house. The two of them together. They had a lot to talk about.